Enemy Past

By

Matthew Laird

Stacey —
Thanks for taking the time to read my book. Much appreciated. It was my pleasure to work with you @ HP. I'm confident your leadership will be sorely missed here, but welcome @ SFO. Take care & enjoy!!

Text copyright © 2014 Matthew Laird
All Rights Reserved

This book is dedicated to the memory of Howard K. Brooks. Howard, thank you for providing me with the inspiration and strength to pen my first novel. I would also like to thank my loving wife and best friend Nancy, and my son Brendan for their patience and support.

Table of Contents

Chapter 1
Chapter 2
Chapter 3
Chapter 4
Chapter 5
Chapter 6
Chapter 7
Chapter 8
Chapter 9
Chapter 10
Chapter 11
Chapter 12
Chapter 13
Chapter 14
Chapter 15
Chapter 16
Chapter 17
Chapter 18
Chapter 19
Chapter 20
Chapter 21
Chapter 22
Chapter 23
Chapter 24
Chapter 25
Chapter 26
Chapter 27
Chapter 28
Chapter 29
Chapter 30
Chapter 31
Chapter 32
Chapter 33
Chapter 34
Chapter 35
Chapter 36
Chapter 37
Chapter 38
Chapter 39
Chapter 40
Chapter 41
Chapter 42
Chapter 43
Chapter 44
Chapter 45
Chapter 46
Chapter 47
Chapter 48
Chapter 49
Chapter 50
Chapter 51
Chapter 52
Chapter 53
Chapter 54
Chapter 55
Chapter 56
Chapter 57
Chapter 58
Chapter 59
Chapter 60
Chapter 61
Chapter 62
Chapter 63
Chapter 64
Chapter 65
Chapter 66
Chapter 67
Chapter 68
Chapter 69
Chapter 70

Chapter 1
Ocala, Florida
1985

For the most part, retirement had been what everyone promised. Howard could now devote more time to his lovely wife Fran, their son Brendan, and life in general; all things which had been frequently postponed due to his busy career. Good days were defined by leisurely weekend visits to St. Augustine, taking in some spring training baseball in St. Petersburg, or playing cards and enjoying drinks with neighbors on each others' lanais. Great days were defined by semi-annual excursions to New Jersey to visit Brendan and the grandkids, or when Brendan's family came south on vacation trips to visit Grandma and Grandpa, and the Mouse. Almost every day started with a brisk walk through the newly built Oak Run retirement community or time in the gym. This was followed by downing some very strong coffee, while poring over the local newspaper, The New York Times, and a subscription to The New Yorker; all holdovers from what now seemed like a lifetime ago. A little work in his garage workshop, a regularly scheduled early afternoon nap, and an evening Guinness or two normally rounded out the day.

Howard sat in his den at a large mahogany desk which he had built himself from reclaimed lumber. A sofa bed, which came in handy when Brendan and his boys visited, sat opposite, and memorabilia he had collected over the years during his business travels and vacations abroad with Fran filled the cozy space. Howard sat back in his leather chair, staring at the wall which displayed awards and certifications, photos of close colleagues and family, and a few framed prints, including an old and well used map of the New York University campus in Washington Square. Even with a rare afternoon vodka gimlet in hand, Howard found real and deep relaxation elusive, never quite losing the alertness that comes with a career spent dedicated to one's country.

Howard K. Brooks had served nearly 25 years in the FBI, a majority of them in the New York Office, honing an expertise in Counterespionage work. Few men could say they spent longer careers in New York, yet alone in Counterespionage. It wasn't for everyone, as success was measured in esoteric terms and outside the public's general knowledge. Even fellow agents in the "headline grabbing" Criminal program rarely knew of the day to day workings within Counterespionage.

For the most part, Howard had adjusted to retirement. But in those quiet moments when Fran was out shopping with girlfriends old and new, or tending to her numerous flower beds, when Howard was otherwise alone and without distraction, a nagging feeling crept into his semiconscious state just below the surface. Howard had suffered with this disease of the mind for several years, suppressing it with busy work, hoping exhaustion would win the day and he would find himself untethered and free. Howard had identified the trouble years ago, trying to convince himself time and time again that it was beyond his control then and now. At times, he was successful, enjoying days and sometimes weeks free of the symptom. Keeping busy was the best prescription, but Howard failed for the large part, unable to find closure.

"Howard, Howard," Fran repeated. "Are you in your office? Howard, the phone," Fran yelled from the kitchen down the hall. Fran had developed an expertise at holding conversations from other rooms, a skill crafted from years raising their only son. "Howard," Fran called again, refusing to actually walk the few paces between the kitchen and his office.

Howard could hear something unknown but familiar, pulling him from the blissful moment between an afternoon siesta and full alertness. He felt cheated from the elusive and temporary reprieve afforded him through an afternoon catnap, but at the same time, grateful he could file away the nagging feeling. Howard opened his eyes to see Fran standing in the doorway, beautiful as the day they first met.

"Fran, I'm sorry Babe," a term of endearment Howard had assigned to Fran over thirty years prior. "You know I only have half my hearing." Fran had the look of a woman who refused to be ignored.

"Howard, Tom Conrad was on the phone from Washington. He said it wasn't urgent, but asked that you call him back this afternoon if possible."

"Okay Babe, I will," Howard said as he kissed Fran on the cheek and walked past towards the kitchen. Howard grabbed a beer and stretched the phone cord out onto the lanai. Sitting down, Howard dialed the FBI Headquarters switchboard and asked for Tom. Tom's secretary Jan picked up on the second ring.

"Well, hello Howard. Good to hear your voice. Tom will be expecting your call."

"How are John and the boys, Jan?" Howard asked his former secretary. "Did John Jr. finally ask what's her name to marry him?" Howard teased.

"Oh, you know, Howard. You can't rush kids these days. Johnny is still working in Senator Williams' office and attending Georgetown Law School, in his final year. The senior John is his grumpy old self as usual, and Mary will graduate high school this year. How is Fran, Howard? Still putting up with your antics?"

"Yes, my lovely bride seems resigned to the fact that we are married," Howard joked. "Well Jan, better not keep the boss waiting." Jan noted Howard's somewhat bitter voice inflection for the term "boss."

"Seems odd every time you say that, Howard. I still can't get used to the role reversal," Jan offered, as she reflected on old times when Tom referred to Howard as the boss. "I'll put you through. Take care of yourself and don't let Fran get away."

"I won't Jan. I work on it every day. Take care yourself too," Howard replied as Jan announced his call to Tom and transferred the connection.

"Hello Howard, I'm glad you decided to call me back. I thought you would make me wait a day or two," Tom said, his greeting even toned, lacking emotion.

"What, Tom?" Howard paused, "we aren't going to start with a few 'how are you's' and other standard pleasantries?" Howard retorted.

"Well, Howard, Fran brought me up to date if you most know. Said retirement was treating you well, even if you haven't fully embraced it just yet. Sorry Howard, that was a bit rude," Tom continued with a perceptible change in tone. "Let's start over shall we? I would like to ask a favor. Two agents from Gail's old group have requested to interview you about some unfinished business. They seem to think the files may not contain all the back stories on a few unresolved cases and that you may be able to shed some light, perhaps generate a lead or two," Tom explained.

At the mention of Gail's name, Howard drifted off for a moment or two, contemplating the work they had done over the years. Before her retirement, Gail had led a group which kept a constant vigil over unresolved counterespionage anomalies; in other words, operations that had gone badly without logical explanation. Gail and her group were "mole" hunters, dedicated to identifying those who had betrayed the very oath they swore to uphold, an oath to protect the Constitution, and the American people from enemies abroad and enemies within. No one carried that awesome responsibility and bore the weight of the watchful eyes of the competing intelligence agencies more than Gail. Gail was a rare find, possessing both a keen intellect and a dogged determination to leave no stone left unturned.

"Happy to help, Tom, but not so inclined to travel to Washington," Howard replied with a lighter tone in an attempt to accept Tom's strained apology. Animosity had been a stalwart of Tom and Howard's relationship over the past few years. An unfortunate trend, given the past relationship in which Howard had mentored Tom throughout his career, and had even recommended Tom as the prime candidate for

Howard's position of Assistant Director of Counterespionage, a position Howard had briefly, and somewhat reluctantly held before retirement.

"That won't be necessary Howard. Special Agents Mike Gallow and Ed Kowolski can travel down to see you at your convenience. Perhaps it would be best if I have them call you directly for arrangements," Tom offered.

"That would be fine, Tom. I am sincere about being happy to help," Howard replied.

"Very good, Howard, I will pass on your acceptance to the group. You should hear from them in the next day or two. Take care of yourself and Fran, Howard," Tom exclaimed with slight sincerity, at least towards Fran.

"Same to you, Tom," Howard retorted as he hung up the phone without additional fanfare.

Chapter 2
Ocala, Florida
1985

Howard called ahead to the front gate at his retirement community, providing the security guard with the names of Agents Gallow and Kowolski. On time like all good agents, they pulled up out front wearing dark suits and ties, not well suited for the hot Florida sun. Fran greeted both and showed them to the lanai where Howard waited, lost in The Fourth Protocol, a novel written by Frederick Forsyth which Fran had given Howard this past Christmas. An interesting read, Howard felt, if not a bit too dramatic.

"Howard, Agents Gallow and Kowolski are here to see you," Fran announced. Howard put the book down and rose to greet both, extending a friendly hand.

"Mr. Brooks, thank you for agreeing to take the time to see us," said Agent Gallow. "I hope we aren't too much trouble," added Agent Kowolski.

"Nonsense gentlemen, I could use a good distraction. And please, call me Howard."

"Well, thank you again Mr., I mean Howard," Gallow replied catching himself, still not comfortable calling the former assistant director by his first name.

"Please be seated, gentlemen," Howard said pointing to a loveseat near his La-Z-Boy. And before Howard could ask, Fran brought in a tray with glasses full of iced tea for the group. "Thank you, Babe," Howard said to Fran, causing both Gallow and Kowolski to exchange grins. "So, I understand you two work in the Special Projects group. How can I help?"

"Howard, you would know our mission better than anyone. After all, you created the group back in the 1970s", Gallow offered.

"Unfortunately, we had no choice. Such groups only serve one purpose, and in all cases, positive results are negative for the Bureau and our country," Howard explained with melancholy.

"Couldn't agree more," replied Kowolski. "Working in the group is professionally rewarding but at the same time, it's distasteful business." Kowolski continued, "Howard, we are following one of the threads behind why you and Gail had started the group in the first place. We've read all the files, including the assessment pieces authored by Gail, but we can't help but wonder if we are missing something. I know this might be a bit painful for you, but can you recount for us the details behind Operation RED EYE from the beginning. We are hoping some obscure detail will emerge, creating additional leads to which we can focus our efforts."

With the mention of Operation RED EYE, Howard slouched slightly in his chair as Gallow and Kowolski had keyed on the nagging feeling which often crept into Howard's mind during those quiet times. "Well gentlemen, I would suggest you refill your glasses and loosen your ties. We have a bit of ground to cover," Howard remarked as his words and eyes drifted off into the distance, no one in the room knowing yet that 1985 would become known as the "Year of the Spy."

Chapter 3
Framlingham 153
Parham, England
February 14, 1945

Most days were the same. They started with an early wake up call, a full breakfast with fresh eggs and often ham, the makings of a last meal. Briefing reports, good wishes from the Squadron Commander, pre-flight checklists, and moments of quiet reflection followed before the four powerful Wright Cyclone engines were sparked to life. Most days ended the same. Welcome home greetings from your Crew Chief, post-mission briefings where the fate of brethren was learned, light chow, and frequent visits to the local Glemham House pub for a few pints. Toasts followed by moments of silence for those that didn't return were painfully regular. If the mood was light, maybe a profitable game of darts or poker could be found. All days reminded one of the ever-present threats of violence and death. All nights were filled with reflections of friends lost to that day's mission. These were the days of war, when young boys became men in foreign lands, on exotic seas, and in the heavens far from home.

Technical Sgt. Howard K. Brooks, a small town kid from the very small town of Otho, Iowa, finished his pre-flight checklist and strapped himself into his radio operator's seat. He plugged in the electric cord attached to his sheepskin and leather flight suit, an absolute necessity when flying at high altitudes in the winter's cold where temperatures often reached 30 to 50 degrees below zero Fahrenheit. He radioed his readiness to the flight crew.

Howard was on his 28th mission aboard Crew 64's main instrument of war, the Liberty Belle. The old girl was as rock steady as they came. Her capable crew had been together since their training in Avon, Florida. The crew picked up a new B-17 in Savanna, Georgia, and ferried the airplane to Wales, with stops at Manchester, New Hampshire, Goose Bay, Labrador and Keflavic, Iceland. On October 1, 1944, Howard and the rest of Crew 64 were assigned to Framlingham 153, home of the 390th Bomber Group of the 8th Army Air Force. The Liberty Belle was assigned their steed. Today, February 14, 1945, the 390th had originally been scheduled to participate in a bombing run to Dresden, Germany that morning, but for unknown and fateful reasons, had been diverted to Cheb, Czechoslovakia. Cheb was on the border of Germany and Czechoslovakia, about 30 or 40 miles southwest of Dresden. The crew didn't mind nor care, each mission held the same odds of success or failure, life or death, and it was their job.

The Liberty Belle waited her turn on the runway, lifted off, and climbed to 10,000 feet. Leif Halvorson, the crew's navigator, came up on the interphone, "10,000 feet, everyone on oxygen." For the duration of the mission, every five minutes Halvorsen would repeat his call for an "oxygen check." Each check started at the front and worked its way back: "Bombardier okay," "Pilot okay," "Co-pilot okay," "Top turret okay," "Radio okay," "Ball turret okay," "Waist okay," "Tail okay." She would eventually climb to 25,000 feet, and at that altitude, death would visit in a few minutes without oxygen.

Howard's position in the forward fuselage, along with the small window he could use from his seated position, gave him a great view of the assembling planes of his 570th Bomber Squadron. When the lead airplane of the 570th BS got close to assembly altitude, they started firing colored flares. Each flare had either two or three fireballs with different combinations of red, green and yellow. Each group leader fired a different color. There were flares everywhere, and to Howard, in the early dawn, it looked like the 4th of July. When the Liberty Belle spotted its lead plane, she started cutting corners to catch up. Similar maneuvers eventually got everyone into a tight formation.

The lead airplane continued to fly the racetrack pattern and climb. Fuel in the "Tokyo" tanks was emptied into the main tanks. The Tokyo tanks had been added to each wing tip and held 500 gallons each of precious fuel and increased the airplane's range by about 40%. When Liberty Belle Pilot Donald Hassig and Co-pilot Howard Sackett determined enough fuel had been burned from the main tanks, Howard was told to open the valves. He performed this task from the radio room by pulling up on two handles that were attached to cables which ran through the wings to the valves. When opened, the fuel drained by gravity into the main tanks. Howard then pulled two other handles. This action closed the valves while opening others; one in the leading edge of each wing and one in the trailing edge, allowing air from outside to flow through the Tokyo tanks to clear out the fumes. Howard knew that although it was a simple procedure, if he didn't do it correctly, the Tokyo tanks would become full of fumes and, like bombs, could be ignited by a bullet or anything else. More potential for death, as if flying into enemy airspace wasn't enough.

At the appointed time, each bomber group headed east, in turn, from a pre-determined point on the east coast of England and continued to climb until reaching the bombing altitude, which was usually about 25,000 feet. When halfway across the North Sea, the gunners test fired their .50 caliber air cooled guns one by one in short bursts of five or six rounds. Crew 64 wanted to be sure all guns were working properly, but didn't want to waste ammo that would most likely be needed later. Although Howard's primary assignment was his Radio Operator's duties, he was also cross-trained as a gunner.

Shortly after, Bombardier Don McConnell moved from the Liberty Belle's nose and into the bomb bay to remove the safety pins from the bombs and arm the bombs. They were soft metal cotter-key type pins that went through matching holes in two pieces of metal on each bomb. These pins prevented the propeller wheels, one on the nose of the bomb and one on the tail, from spinning off in case the bomb was dropped, accidentally or otherwise, while over friendly territory. Don put the pins in his pocket so they could be reinserted in case the crew had to bring back some or all of the bombs. Around this same time, the Liberty Belle crossed the coastline, and P-51 fighter escorts could be seen, in several groups of four, giving comfort to all aboard. Even on a long mission like a run to Cheb, the bomber group's "little friends" could escort the group to the target and back.

It was a beautiful, clear day, where you could see forever. While Hassig and Sackett were flying over rivers, highways, railroads, towns and villages, only the scenery could be seen from their eagle's perch so high above. To Howard and the crew, there was nothing to indicate that the biggest, bloodiest war ever was going on down below. Howard couldn't help but think of those poor guys down there in the snow and mud, and he knew it didn't look pretty to them. All aboard knew that although their bombing missions were far from pleasant, and downright scary at times, their days were marked by a few hours at a time, before a return home to a hot meal, a dry, warm bed, and no worries about anyone trying to sneak up on them. The men on the ground were out in the weather 24 hours a day. They were wet and cold, and only got a couple of cold "K ration" meals a day, if they were lucky. Many in the crew had brothers down there somewhere, and all knew that as bad as their days could get, the men on the ground were far worse off.

The bomber group finally reached its IP (initial point), where the bomb run begins, and flak bursts from German 88's could be seen ahead as small black puffs of smoke. When the lead plane opened its bomb bay doors, so did everybody else as they continued toward the target. The bomb run, as usual, was about five minutes long, and flak shells were exploding all around. Fortunately, none came close and the Liberty Belle sustained no known damage. When the lead plane's bombs dropped, McConnell announced, "Bombs away" and hit his switch releasing the Liberty Belle's arsenal. Howard could definitely feel it when 5,000 pounds of bombs were released all at once and the Liberty Belle jumped in altitude. Howard opened the door between the radio compartment and the bomb bay, took a look, and said, "All bombs gone," prompting McConnell to close the bomb bay doors. The lead plane made a small turn to the left and descended about 200 feet, hoping to throw off the German gunners' aim. The lead plane then made a long right turn and headed west, back toward England. Co-pilot Howard Sackett, better known to the crew as "Howie," reduced the prop RPM to cruise setting and put the mixture controls into auto lean. The controls had been set at the climb setting ever since takeoff, but now, with the bombs gone and about 2/3 of the fuel burned, the airplane was about 15,000 pounds lighter than it was at takeoff.

Howard and the rest of Crew 64 settled down for what he hoped would be a boring 2-1/2 to 3 hour ride home. About 45 minutes after their bombs were delivered and their turn for home was made, a few flak bursts materialized to the left of a B-17 group, three groups in front of the 390th's sortie. Hassig and Sackett could see the smoke from the exploding shells leaning to the right, which meant they were being fired from somewhere on the left. As a result, Howard felt the Liberty Belle tilt slightly to the right as the trailing groups, one by one, moved in response. The flak kept coming, so the 390th's lead plane continued veering right. However, this last move put the Liberty Belle's crew and her sister ships within range of additional German guns, setting a trap.

Chapter 4
Over Germany
February 14, 1945

Darkness and drifting were abruptly replaced by the violent shaking of metal, the sounds of straining engines, and a strong smell of gas filling the Liberty Belle's fuselage. Although his normally acute senses were astonishingly dull, Howard realized he was no longer sitting upright in his radio operator's chair. Instead, he was supine and having difficulty breathing. As the Liberty Belle broke through the clouds of flak, Howard's brief moments of consciousness were also marked by barely audible soft moans and cries for help from fellow injured crew. Not cognizant of the time, Howard was unaware of when the Liberty Belle had broken from formation after delivering its payload over Cheb, but even in his reduced state he sensed catastrophe had struck.

The Liberty Belle had taken an enormous beating from German flak while on the return leg of the bombing run. Flak had destroyed the tail's vertical stabilizer and rudder, and all of the right horizontal stabilizer and elevator. Adding insult to injury, the landing gear extended permanently, the entire electrical system failed, and gasoline leaked into the lower fuselage from the right wing area. The old girl fell out of formation unable to maintain altitude or airspeed with the gear down, and it became a fight to keep her afloat, marked by the sheer will of Hassig and Sackett to save what remained of Crew 64. It was Crew 64's 28th mission, and the odds had finally caught up with them. Waist gunner John Cullen was now on his way to the heavens, and Antoine Mercier, the top turret gunner, would never fight again as a result of a large piece of shrapnel that penetrated through his upper arm about halfway between his elbow and his shoulder. Howard's last memory aboard was the soothing sound of his navigator's voice. Then he was consumed by darkness and the sense of drifting once again.

Chapter 5
U.S. Military Hospital
Outside London, England
April 02, 1945

Recovery at the 15th General Hospital near Liege, Belgium, led to an even longer recovery stint at a Convalescent Center in Warwickshire, England. Nearly two months had passed since Hassig had expertly guided the barely airworthy Liberty Belle to an Allied fighter base, the Le Culot A-89 Airfield south of Beauvechain, Belgium. The old girl's tenure in battle had been just over a year, with 64 missions over enemy territory. Now she would never fly again. The Liberty Belle's serviceable parts were cannibalized, and the rest lost to history.

Howard was now separated from the family he had grown with since Crew 64's formation in March 1944. Their journey together from crew formation in Avon, Florida, and through Hunter Field in Savannah, Georgia, before debarking overseas was now at its end. During peace time, life at Framlingham 153 would have been ideal with its picturesque landscapes, nearby quaint villages, Sunday service at St. Michael the Archangel, known to village residents as St. Mike's, and its Norman castle. But all of this and the graciousness of the area's lovely locals could not conceal a world at war, and a nagging sense of fatality was omnipresent. Howard flew his first mission with Crew 64 on 10/06/1944 and his last on 02/14/1945. He had survived, but his recovery would be long and lonely. During recovery, the endless days were filled with reflection on the new friends he had made and uncertainty about his future. Mae was always on his mind.

At the age of twenty-one, Technical Sergeant Howard K. Brooks enlisted in the U.S. Army Air Corps in February 1941, prior to the United States' entry into World War II. The jobs of working in the gypsum mill near Fort Dodge like his father, or the grain elevator like so many others, could not hold Howard's attention. Economics in a small farming community only reinforced his decision to join the Army Air Corps.

Growing up in Iowa, Howard was very athletic and academically bright. In high school, he played basketball and competed in Golden Gloves boxing, winning many matches with his sneaky right cross. As a boy, Howard developed a fascination with the wonders of shortwave radio, and ordered his first Aero Short Wave set at the age of 10. He could often be found studying Morse code, tinkering with radio tubes manufactured by Neotron, and re-reading dog eared and worn copies of amateur radio magazines. Howard found that he could explore a vast world through his radio set, often tapping out messages day and night to stations in Mexico City, Leningrad and Tokyo. The lure of exotic lands and bustling metropolises pulled at Howard's sensibilities. Call it destiny, God's plan, or fate, even at a young age, Howard knew this draw would take him from his family's humble homestead and into the larger world to find his way.

Howard enlisted at Fort Des Moines where he took the Army General Classification Test. Like many young men of his age, Howard had a desire to fly fighter planes or bombers. Howard tested strong demonstrating a keen aptitude, however, his slight color blindness kept him out of pilot training. So, Howard was sent off to basic Army training, which he found to be a manageable challenge. After basic, Howard was trained as a parachute systems rigger. However, all things changed that December with the attack on Pearl Harbor, and America's declaration of war. Howard's keen mind, restless nature, and longing for adventure fueled his desire to seek a greater role and deployment overseas. Like many young men of the time, such as his older brother Clarence who would serve in the U.S. Navy, personal risk and peril were distant thoughts as Howard was determined to fight this war in the air, one way or another.

    With his affinity for amateur short wave radio, it was natural for Howard to seek out training as a Radio Operator. An assignment aboard a B-17 Flying Fortress would ensure he made it overseas. Training as a gunner came with the position, and increased his chances of making a direct impact. Howard was reassigned to the Sioux Falls Army Air Force Technical Training Command and its Radio Training School in South Dakota. During the 26 week course, Howard received official training on Morse code and radio theory, and learned how to identify enemy aircraft, often claiming the highest scores in his class. While assigned to the base, Howard filled his little downtime by keeping his boxing skills sharp, and like so many seeking companionship, he frequently attended dances held at the Arkota Ballroom. One evening, a small town kid from Otho, Iowa, met a wonderful local girl named Mae. Like many of their time, their courtship was brief and urgent. Struck by love, they discussed marriage in late September 1944, days before Howard's departure for England. But Howard felt it best to leave with a promise to return, not wanting to leave Mae a young war bride and potential widow.

As Howard lied back with his eyes closed, drifting in and out, his thoughts of Mae, their homecoming and future, were interrupted by a friendly and welcoming voice. "Howard, you awake? Its Don, Don Hassig." Howard blinked his eyes open, breaking the fog, and looked into the smiling and paternal eyes of Hassig. Although they were roughly the same age, Don's official but natural role as the crew's leader caused his men to look up to him as a son would to his father. Hassig was seated next to Howard on a stool reserved for the visiting doctor.

"Lieutenant Hassig, what a sight for sore eyes, and an aching backside I must admit," Howard exclaimed as he began to hunch himself up on his elbows. Hassig helped him up and repositioned the bed's pillows as Howard leaned back.

"That would be Captain Hassig, Sergeant Brooks".

"Sorry, Lieutenant, I mean Captain. Congratulations to you. When did you receive the promotion?" Howard asked as he cleared his head.

"Well Howard, apparently the Air Force has a pretty short memory, forgetting I lost one of their very expensive war birds," Hassig teased. "The promotion came in about a month later. How are you feeling?"

"Pretty good for losing a good portion of my most admirable feature," Howard jested. "The Doc said that my backside will eventually fill in, but I may have a permanent divot. My right arm was fractured in two places, but should heal fine. The concussion and damage to my scalp was the worst of it. I couldn't see straight nor could I sit up without my world spinning for the better part of three weeks. The Doc said I was lucky it was a cold weather run, as the leather head cover slowed the shrapnel and prevented it from penetrating deeper," Howard exclaimed. In reality, Howard downplayed the constant fog he felt since awaking in the hospital. His normally keen mind felt slow and murky. The doctors told him only time would tell if the feeling would be short or long-term.

"Well, you just take it easy and listen to the doctors. By the time you are cleared for flight duty, this war will be over. In March, our ground forces advanced over the Rhine and moved well into Germany. Our flights have been cut back a bit, but the crew reached our 35th mission, Howard. Our part of this war is over, and we are going home soon. I can't imagine you will be far behind. The boys miss you, Howard, and send their best," Hassig remarked, fighting the wave of melancholy building in his throat.

Howard replied, "I miss the guys also. Can't believe this may be over soon. Captain, I'm real fuzzy on what happened. Yeah, I know we flew into a big field of flak, but the rest of it... The Doc told me the concussion explains most of my memory lapse, but he told me most will come back in due time. What happened? Was I the only one hit?"

Howard watched Hassig walk to the foot of the bed, his chin hung low towards his chest as he turned back towards Howard, quiet, too quiet, even for Hassig. After what seemed like a few minutes, Hassig found his voice.

"Howard, we took a hell of a beating. Shells exploded all around the Ol' Belle. She pitched up and the rudder pedals lost all tension. They were just hanging free. I reached for the elevator trim control and gave it a big turn, but it did nothing. In fact, it turned so easily, it was obvious that the cables had been cut and it was no longer attached to the elevator. The radio and interphone were also dead, so we had no way to talk to each other except to shout, and we had no radio to talk to anyone else. At the same time, I heard the landing gear extending, so I looked out the window to make sure and could see that the left wheel was all the way down. I asked Howie to look on his side and the right one was down too. We moved the control switch back and forth several times, but the wheels stayed down.

"Mercier stepped down from his top turret perch and said that he had been hit in the left arm. He was obviously in pain and his arm just hung there. About that time, Halvorsen and McConnell came crawling up from the nose compartment to see what was going on. They had their chutes with them, and one of them asked, 'Are we going to bail out?' I said, 'No, at least, not right now.' I told them that all four engines seemed to be okay. Some control cables were obviously cut, but I thought we could control it and would attempt to keep going. We had already fallen out of formation because we could not maintain altitude or airspeed with the gear down. I asked Leif if he knew where we were and he did. So I told him to keep track of our position, that for now, at least, we would stay under the stream of bombers. I also told him to try to find us an airport as soon as possible after we crossed the front lines.

"I then told McConnell to do whatever he could for Mercier, who had a piece of shrapnel go through his upper arm, about halfway between his elbow and his shoulder. About all he could do was secure a bandage on his arm and give him a morphine shot to help ease the pain. I think McConnell put a tourniquet on it until he got it bandaged to slow down the bleeding. Then he taped a splint to the arm to keep it from moving around too much.

"It wasn't easy to keep the nose down on the plane, but one man could do it, so Howie and I took turns. About then, I looked back and saw Garcia and Surma come through the door from the bomb bay, up from their ball turret and the tail gunner positions. Surma was wearing a backpack parachute and Garcia had his chest pack with him. They were each carrying a walk-around oxygen bottle. This was actually no more than two or three minutes after the flak hit, so I asked if they were okay. Garcia said, 'Yes,' and so I asked if either knew how to crank up the landing gear. Garcia said that he did, so I said, 'Get the crank and try it. I doubt that it will come up, but try.' I told them to get you and John Cullen if they needed help. That's when Garcia told me about Cullen. Howard, John was killed by the flak and you were hurt real bad. I said to Garcia, 'Are you sure?' and without hesitation he said, 'Yes, I'm sure.' I looked to Surma and he nodded in agreement.

"Obviously, there was nothing more I could do about Cullen, so I told Surma to tend to you and told Garcia to work on cranking up the gear. Garcia tried but he couldn't budge it, which didn't surprise me. So I told him to put the crank away, but stay in the cockpit. There was nothing they could do in the back, and we couldn't talk to them if they were back there. We were still at 24,000 feet or so and still needed oxygen, so we had to pull off our masks to talk.

"About that time, one of the guys from the nose compartment stuck his head up from the tunnel below the cockpit and said, 'There is a stream of gasoline running into the tunnel from the right side.' I asked how big a stream it was, and he said it was small, but it had already made a puddle at the bottom. This, of course, was not good news, but again, there was nothing we could do about it. I'm sure we were lucky that the entire electrical system was knocked out, because any of the several electric motors, switches, relays, etc., in that area could have produced sparks and ignited the gas, blowing up the airplane. The air speed indicator, altimeter and most engine instruments needed no electricity, so they were working, but we had no fuel quantity gauges. We knew about how much fuel we had when all this started, but we also knew that we were losing some inside the airplane and might be losing even more on the outside. I told Halvorsen to find us an airport as soon as possible.

"We had been flying at 150 MPH indicated air speed while in formation, but now, with the gear down, we slowed to 140. We left the power where it was so as not to use more fuel than necessary in case we did have leaks that we didn't know about. At first we were losing about 200 feet per minute, but as we lost altitude it improved. We kept plodding along, and after a little more than an hour, Halvorsen said that we were approaching the front lines. We were still at 15,000 feet, and pretty well able to hold altitude, but we wanted to be sure we didn't get too low where there might be fighting going on. Someone on the ground might decide to take a shot at us and we had already been through enough.

"When Halvorsen was sure we had crossed the lines, we pulled the power back and started descending a bit faster. Halvorsen said there was a U.S. fighter base showing on his map a few miles ahead, so we headed for it. When we had it in sight, we continued our descent and circled the field. One of the guys fired a few red flares to indicate that we had wounded aboard. The tower gave us a green light and we were cleared to land. Everyone, except for Howie and myself, went to the radio compartment and sat on the floor with their backs against the forward wall. Garcia tried to make you as comfortable as possible, and Surma kept busy trying to stop the bleeding.

"We didn't expect any trouble from the landing, but since we had no way of knowing just how much damage had been done to the airplane, they assumed the ditching position. I told them to stay in that position until we were definitely on the ground and slowing down, then to get to the entrance door, open it, and jump out as soon as we were slow enough. We didn't want anyone to get hurt now, when we had just about made it. Mercier, even though he was injured, was with them.

"They fastened the two doors open at each end of the bomb bay so we could give a yell just before touchdown. Sackett and I went over what we were going to do. We had hydraulic pressure, so the brakes should work, but we had no way to apply them. They were usually applied by pressing on the top of the rudder pedals with your toes, but the rudder pedals were just hanging limp and we couldn't reach far enough forward to put any pressure on them. We decided that as soon as we got the airplane on the ground, we would make sure that it was heading off the runway, then Howie would cut the mixture controls and I would turn off the ignition switches and we would get out of there as fast as possible.

"As we headed down the final approach, we were both holding the yoke forward, Howie with both hands and me with my left hand as I was controlling the throttles with my right. Just before the runway, we were letting the yoke come back slowly to raise the nose and decrease airspeed. Before we touched down, the yoke lost all tension and came all the way back. The airplane touched down a few seconds later and actually made a smooth landing. It all worked just like we planned.

"We were now going down the runway with no means of control except for the throttles. It was almost like the airplane knew what it was supposed to do. It slowly started drifting left, off the runway, and I said, 'Cut them.' Howie turned off the mixture controls and I turned off the ignition switches. He then unfastened his seat belt, headed for the tunnel below the cockpit, and opened the hatch. The airplane was moving slowly, so he jumped out, with me right behind him. The rest of the crew was already out and standing behind the plane. They had dragged you off with them, Howard, unconscious.

"When the airplane had gone off the runway, it was sinking a couple of inches into the dirt. It hadn't rolled very far, but it was well enough off the runway so it wouldn't interfere with the operation of the field. About the time we got out, a fire truck, a Jeep, and two ambulances came driving up. We turned you and Mercier over to the crew on one of them. They put you guys on litters, shoved you into an ambulance, and took off. I told them that there was one more inside who was beyond help. Four guys jumped into the plane. After a while, they came out carrying a litter that held Cullen's blanket-covered body. They put him into the other ambulance and one of them said, 'He was obviously killed immediately and never knew what hit him.' Thank God for that anyways."

"We started looking over the Liberty Belle. Her control surfaces were covered with doped fabric, and the rudder and right elevator had all of the fabric stripped off. There was nothing left but the framework. There were hundreds of various sized holes in the fuselage, vertical fin, right horizontal stabilizer, and right wing. There were some holes on the left side where pieces of flak had gone all the way through and come out the other side. There was one hole in the wing about four inches in diameter which we thought could only have been made by an 88mm shell going through, but it hadn't exploded. She was a pretty sad looking airplane, but she had taken us to safety. We felt a lot of affection for that old bird and we hated to leave her there but, obviously, we couldn't take her with us, wherever we went from there."

Howard sat quietly for a moment, thinking of John Cullen. They had been close, becoming like brothers. All of them had, of course, as war has a way of forging new families. "Where is John at now, Captain? I mean where was he laid to rest?" Howard asked.

"Well Howard, they interned John's body in a U.S. Cemetery back in Belgium called Henri-Chapelle near Liege, not too far from where they took you for medical care. I've been told the War Department can move him back home to the states if his family requests it. Hell, I've never even met his family. Writing that letter to his mom was the hardest thing I've ever done, Howard. I hope to God I never have to write another letter like that again." There was nothing more to say. They had both learned enough over the past few months to know that the only thing certain anymore was that death would knock often and loudly.

Hassig broke the silence. "Howard, don't dwell on John's death, and don't go down the road of asking yourself why him and not you. It won't do anyone any good, especially John. Instead, focus on getting better, getting home to your loved ones, and thinking about what you're going to do next in this crazy world. I'm going to leave you my home address. When you get home, I want you to feel free to reach out at anytime if you need anything, or just want a friend to share a cold one. Howard, the crew and I have placed a lot on your shoulders over the past few months and I've depended on you. I've never had a doubt that you wouldn't perform you duties to the highest level. Let me return the favor someday... And from here out, call me Don."

"Thanks Captain, sorry, Don. I may take you up on that offer someday. I'm going to miss you and the rest of the guys. When you get back to Framlingham, please pass on my best. I'll also give you my address back in Otho. Let me know if you ever make plans to get the crew back together for some darts and a few pints back home," Howard said as he struggled to fight back the tears.

Hassig turned to leave, but stopped and looked back at Howard. "I almost forgot. Otho's in Iowa, right?" Hassig asked with a smile on his face. Howard nodded in the affirmative, and Hassig continued. "I caught a train down here with John Larsen. John, he likes to be called Jack, was the pilot of a B-17 with the 381st BG called the Sleepy Time Gal. He flew us back to England from Belgium. Jack's here at the hospital visiting an English nurse named Betty, supposed to be quite the looker. Jack said she looks a lot like Veronica Lake but most do, don't they?" Hassig said with a wink. "Anyways, he's from Waterloo, which I guess is in Iowa too, right? I asked him to stop by your bed and say, 'Hi.' Jack seems like a real good guy. He just completed his 35th mission, is heading home, and offered to call your folks when he gets back to the states," Hassig explained. "Well Howard, again, take care of yourself and God bless."

"Same to you Don. God speed," Howard called out as Hassig started to walk down the corridor.

Chapter 6
Oder River, Forty-three miles from Berlin
Early February, 1945

Hard won gains made since January 12, exhausted yet exhilarated Lt. Dmitry Borisovich Abramenkov, T-34/85 tank commander, Red Army's 1st Guards Tank Brigade of the 1st Guards Tank Army. In April 1944, at the ripe old age of 19, Dmitry had been entrusted with command of the medium tank and its four man crew. But then again, battle, especially in the Soviet's Red Army, aged boys to men in quick order. Considered one of the Red Army's best, the T-34 could not compete one-on-one with the superior German Panzers and Tigers, but instead, relied on superior numbers and battlefield tactics, something Dmitry had become quite adept. The Red Army's gains made by the 1st Belorussian Fronts during the Vistula–Oder Offensive were accelerating daily. They had moved the Eastern Front over 300 miles from its start at the Vistula River in Poland, to the Oder River, Germany's eastern border and natural boundary between Poland and Germany.

Death was not feared, but expected among men of the Soviet Red Army. Men such as Dmitry Abramenkov did not make plans. Family, education and careers were not an individual's decision. Such life basics were considered matters of the state. As Dmitry's father and two brothers were already dead from this war, the fate of their bodies and souls unknown, he expected the same. He was not afforded time to mourn their deaths. Pausing to handle proper burial and mourning meant little to a populous expected to sacrifice all for the survival of a system in which individual concerns and opinions were not considered. However, privately in the brief pauses between battles and enemy engagements, Dmitry started to sense something. Perhaps it was hope, although a foreign concept at best to Dmitry and a generation who had struggled since birth. He began to think he may survive this war... Thoughts he dared not share with anyone.

As the front moved and German resistance began to wane, Dmitry and his comrades new that Berlin was theirs for the taking, and they pushed hard for the right to unleash ungodly destruction and retribution before the pompous British or ugly Americans could work out their politics. Revenge was for his comrades alone. Much would be exacted on the arrogant Germans.

Chapter 7
U.S. Military Hospital
Outside London, England
April 1945

Howard saw a tall and polished soldier wearing the uniform of a US Army Air Force Captain walking towards him in the space between the beds. As a British nurse turned from her patient and began to walk the opposite way, the captain pivoted his head for a few moments and turned back to continue his walk, a slight smile forming on his well groomed face. The nurse also turned for a moment and took notice of the handsome American officer. The captain's walk was confident and very erect. As he approached Howard's bed, his eyes shifted between the names on clipboards attached to the foot of each bed.

Recognizing Howard's name, the captain stopped, fixed a large smile upon his clean-shaven face and said, "You must be the Sergeant Brooks with the dented derriere I've heard so much about."

Howard could not help being impressed by the captain's confidence and bearing. He exuded command presence, not contrived, but natural. "And you must be Captain Jack Larsen who Don, I'm sorry, Captain Hassig, told me would be stopping by. Captain Hassig said you are from Waterloo, is that correct, Sir?" Howard asked.

"Howard, why don't two small-town kids from Iowa call each other by their first names," Larsen recommended.

"Please, call me Jack. Besides, you can't even stand for a proper solute."

"That sounds just fine Sir, I mean Jack," Howard replied, quickly catching himself and returning Jack's infectious smile.

"How are you feeling Howard?" Jack asked. "Don said you took a hell of a beating coming back from Cheb."

"Well, much better now that I've had a few weeks to recover. I have to admit though, much of what happened that morning isn't fresh in my mind," Howard said as his eyes drifted from Jack's and towards the floor. Howard paused before continuing. "Don just filled me in on what happened to our top turret and one of our waist gunners. All things considered, I'm doing just fine. In fact, I think I'll be cleared for duty in no time at all," Howard remarked, not really confident of his statement.

"I've never suffered from a concussion myself, but from what I understand, short-term memory loss sometimes occurs. The docs told me you might continue to experience bouts of hazy fog and possibly vertigo when you get back on your feet. As you said, all things considered, maybe it's just as well you don't clearly remember what happened. And by the way, don't be in such a hurry to work your way back to your base and into another fortress. If Don did not tell you, we've almost got this thing wrapped up. We are already starting to scale back on bombing missions." Larsen paused for a moment, looked around the immediate area, and leaned in close to Howard. "Can you keep a secret, Howard?" Jack asked rhetorically." "Now we are hearing talk about they want some of us to participate in some sort of large scale food drops over the Netherlands. They are calling it 'Operation Chowhound.' Apparently, the Germans are still capable of disrupting supply lines, and the Dutch are starving. I've been told my crew and I will be flying a couple of these runs before ending our time here and returning home. The boys are a bit upset by having to extend our mission time, but they tell us these are simply milk runs and we should not run into any German fighters or flak there and back," Jack offered.

Changing the subject, Jack asked Howard what he did before the war back in Otho. Howard explained to Jack that he was working on a local family farm and at a granary before joining the Army Air Corps in early 1941. Jack asked, "So what do you intend on doing when you get back?"

Howard thought for a minute, and said, "Well, I guess I can return and go to work with my dad. My dad would expect that of me. But my heart is just not in it. Jack, can you keep a secret? I'm not thrilled about returning to the small town anymore. Besides random death and mayhem, this war has taken me places I only read or dreamed about. I've been hearing a lot about a new program to pay for college for returning soldiers. I think I may take a hard look at that program, and take advantage of it before I become an old man," Howard remarked with a bit of melancholy in his voice as he used his unscathed arm to rub his temples.

Jack laughed in response, noticing Howard's discomfort both physically and emotionally. Howard then asked Jack what he had done before this crazy war started and everyone found themselves living day by day in strange, far-off lands. Jack told Howard that he was a police officer in Waterloo, having been on the force for nearly four years. Jack continued by telling Howard that he attended college at Northwestern University in Chicago. Jack was the first from his family to graduate from college, but not the first in his family to enter law enforcement. Jack's older brother and father were on the force, and it was natural for Jack to follow in their footsteps. As Jack relayed this information to Howard, he privately thought that even though he enjoyed policing, he felt something lacking and that he could do a bit more. The war was a distraction from Jack having to make any important career decisions.

Howard asked Jack if he would be returning to the department when he got back, and Jack replied, "I plan on it. They've held a spot open for me for the last three years since I left for flight training and was deployed to England." Although he had just met Howard, Jack decided to be honest. "You know Howard, I've never told anyone this, but over the last three years, I've been thinking a lot about joining the FBI. A few months before joining up with the Army Air Force, I was working on a kidnapping and homicide case with a couple of FBI agents out of their Minneapolis office. I couldn't help but be impressed by their approach to both the crime scene, and the way they pieced the puzzle together. They were very polished, well trained, and walked with an air of confidence," Jack expressed.

As Jack finished his sentence, the same British nurse who had taken notice of Jack as they brushed by each other, approached the bed next to Howard's. Over the last couple weeks, Howard had avoided looking in that particular soldier's direction. Howard felt guilty he had been in the hospital now for a lengthy amount of time, and that his injuries, although serious, paled in comparison to this soldier's plight. Although

Howard did not know the extent of the soldier's injuries, the full set of bandages wrapped around his face and head, the fact that both his legs were in traction, and the constant flurry of medical staff, were enough clues for Howard to know that he was in a bad way. Hell, Howard had no clue if, in fact, his neighbor next door was a soldier, airman, Marine, or sailor. One quickly learned to develop avoidance mechanisms to ease the pain. Jack barely noticed that Howard had grown quiet, as he occupied his time staring at the well-developed and shapely backside of the young nurse. Jack turned back to Howard and noticed that Howard was also taking in the scenery. Both exchanged smiles, realizing the subject of their common thoughts.

Jack pulled out a small notebook and pencil from his dress jacket and jotted down his home address and telephone exchange. "Howard, once you're settled and have decided whether or not you're going to college or staying at home, give me a call or write me a letter. It would be good to have someone to talk to about shared experiences overseas. And if you need anything, anything at all, don't hesitate to ask," Jack offered.

Jack picked up his aviator's hat from Howard's bed and walked close to Howard's side as he offered his hand. "Howard, take care and don't rush to get back to the 390th. If I was a betting man, I would put my money on the 390th packing up by the time you get back to Framlingham." Howard replied, "That's the second time today I've heard someone say that. Jack, it was very nice to meet you. I won't hesitate to write, and thanks for the offer. You get home safe and don't go getting yourself hurt on any milk runs," Howard said with a smile.

Jack replaced the cover on his head, pulled tightly on the bottom of his tunic, and executed a perfect about-face. As Jack walked away, he couldn't help himself but to take one last look back at the British nurse. Although Howard couldn't see it from his view, he knew that Jack had a wide smile on his face.

Chapter 8
German Side of the Oder River East of Frankfurt
Early Morning, April 1945

Lt. Dmitry Abramenkov and crew had bedded down for the night in relative comfort. The forest floor had thawed sufficiently, and straw from a nearby barn kept the moisture at bay. Close to the front lines, but not as close as the exhausted and hungry infantry, Dmitry closed his eyes, hoping to gain a few precious hours of sleep before the morning's push to surpass Frankfurt. Two of his men stood post.

As he drifted off to the faint sounds of distant and unrelenting artillery fire, intent on burning Frankfurt to the ground, he was suddenly awakened by Sgt. Viktor Viktorovich Kulikov with a slight nudge. "Dmitry, there is movement," Viktor Viktorovich whispered near Dmitry's ear.

Dmitry rose carefully as men of his crew began to stir quietly, also sensing movement beyond the thick wall of pine trees to their west. Although at times undefined and subject to constant change as the Soviet Red Army logged rapid territorial gains, Dmitry and the others knew the front lines should be well west of their location. Not willing to take any chances this late on their road towards victory, Dmitry assembled men from his and another tank crew positioned some fifty meters to their south. Dmitry appointed Sgt. Kulikov as point, and they began their move to investigate. Twenty meters into their advance, Sgt. Kulikov motioned them to a halt, and signaled with his hand towards an area of thick brush.

In broken but passable German, Dmitry challenged the shadows with an air of resignation tinged with exhaustion, "Come out now with your hands on your heads or die where you stand. Either way, your journey's over." At that, a man in civilian clothing stood and stepped from the brush. He was followed by a woman whose face in the pale moonlight was white with fear. Two early teen children were in tow, the girl clinging to her mother.

These were not soldiers, but Dmitry and his crew would again find sleep elusive.

Chapter 9
Framlingham, England
April 25, 1945

By the end of April, Howard was cleared to return to active duty. Howard dressed in his Class A uniform, as delivered by Captain Hassig during his visit a few weeks back. The reflection of the Purple Heart pinned to his tunic as Howard checked himself in the mirror left him a bit in low spirits, as he realized from his roommate of the past few weeks that not all wounds were equal.

On a cool and wet spring morning, Howard boarded a London and Northeast England Railway train at Kings Cross, bound for Framlingham Station, located near Parham in Suffolk, England. Flying its first mission on August 12, 1943, at the height of the air war, flight operations at the 390th's base had slowed remarkably by the time Howard returned. Many of the men Howard had spent the better part of a year with at Fram 153, were already gone on troop ships bound for home. Most demoralizing, Hassig and all of Crew 64 had departed after completing their 35th combat mission, making their way home through Glasgow, Scotland, then to New York City on the Queen Elizabeth.

Howard entered the Group's Administrative Office to report for duty, check on a re-assignment to another flight crew, and to collect his back pay and mail. Howard was eager to finish his mission commitment and start his future. Having survived an extremely close call, Howard felt hope creeping back into his life. The future had been just that, as he had lived day by day, as so many men serving their country abroad. Howard opened the first letter on top of the pile. It was from Mae and held a past date of mid-January 1945. Howard realized he must have failed to pick up his mail before their fateful mission aboard the now ruined Liberty Belle. Howard started out of the building reading the letter as he walked. The words struck him hard and stopped him in his tracks. A wave of vertigo hit Howard and he stumbled on his feet. Howard knew it wasn't from any lingering effects of the concussion. Mae had met someone else; a local Sioux Falls businessman, had fallen in love, and had written to Howard to end their short lived promise for a future together. Howard felt betrayed, yet somewhat liberated. He could now pursue his future unfettered.

As Howard stood, steadier now after the initial shock, and with mixed emotions worn on his face, he saw a familiar and smiling face headed in his direction. "Howard, it's good to see you again. The boys weren't so sure you would make it back to Framlingham before the big show was over," called out Lt. Vincent Black, pilot of the 570th's Merry Max. "When did you get back?"

"Just now, actually," Howard stammered as he transitioned from what he had just read and back to reality. "I caught an early train out of London, and hitched a ride in a Willy from the station. And if you must know Sir, it is good to be walking upright without a breeze blowing up my backside."

Black's laugh in response was deep and genuine. "Great to see your sense of humor wasn't damaged. So, what's your status?"

"Well..." Howard said distantly as he pondered having to return home without the family he had arrived with. "I just learned Captain Hassig, and what was left of our crew, already departed. I thought I would start with my back pay, and check on getting assigned to another crew."

"Howard, we've pretty much stood down all flight ops, flying only limited missions in support of the front lines. Follow me and I'll take you over to Colonel Moller's office, and ask that you get assigned to my crew. We've hit our mission mark and are gearing up to start the journey back home. How would you like that? Getting a start on the rest of your life?" Black more or less suggested than asked. Black's words struck a strong chord with Howard.

"Well Sir," Howard paused before continuing. "I've been laid up in the hospital for just over two months. We were on our 28th mission when it all happened. I need to finish my job here like the rest of the boys," Howard stated with a confident voice tinged with a bit of underlying guilt.

"Howard, that's nonsense. You've done more than enough. Be happy you even have the ability to return to normal life, whatever that means to you. Take my advice and walk with me over to the operations building to see the Colonel's staff. And then, let's go home," Black said as a father would to a son, despite their close ages.

And that was it. Howard took Black's advice, joined up with him and his crew, and they followed a journey, similar to that taken by what remained of Crew 64, back to the states. It was the first week of May 1945, and the 390th would soon fly its last mission, then abandon Framlingham 153 as quickly as it had arrived amid the fury of a storm known as the Second World War.

In July 1943, the air echelon of the 390th Bomber Group was dispatched to Framlingham 153 to establish operations. Between that July and May 1945, the 390th had participated in 301 missions, dropping over 19,000 tons of bombs. One hundred and seventy-nine of its aircraft were lost, with 147 missing in action, and 32 lost to other causes. The group's gunners assigned to their mighty Flying Fortresses tallied 378 aircraft destroyed, 78 as "probably" destroyed, and 97 as damaged. The 390th was awarded two Presidential Unit Citations, eight Battle Streamers, and many commendations. During its combat history, the Group's bombing accuracy was reported as best in the 8th Air Force, and its aircraft losses were the lowest per missions flown/bombs dropped. Many would later be asked "What was it like?" For many who had served at Framlingham, losses of friends and comrades would bear heavy on their hearts. But for many, they "Never had it so good."

Chapter 10
April 16, 1945
0330 hours
Polish Side of the Oder River

Dmitry entered the farm's barn, the only building remaining mostly intact in a sea of destruction. The floor was mainly bare and devoid of life, its former inhabitants either killed by artillery or by hungry Soviet or German soldiers. Dmitry and Sgt. Kulikov, having left the remainder of their crew alone to salvage a few precious moments of sleep, personally escorted their prisoners to a temporary Red Army Headquarters station. Kulikov was ordered to remain outside.

"Lt. Abramenkov, why is you chose to leave your post and awaken me at such an inconvenient hour?" remarked Colonel Sergei Matveevich Shtemenko of the Main Intelligence Directorate of the General Staff of the Armed Forces of the Soviet Union.

"My apologies Colonel Shtemenko, it was not my intention. My plan was to deliver the prisoners, return to my men, and drive to Berlin by sundown this evening," Dmitry offered evenly devoid of emotion, not sure as why he was called to meet a high ranking member of the Glavnoye Razvedyvatel'noye Upravleniye, or GRU, the Soviet Union's Military Intelligence Service.

"Your confidence is reassuring Lieutenant. Tell me, why did you not just shoot these civilians where you found them instead of seeing to their personal delivery?"

Not sure of where this line of questioning would lead, including the possibility he would face a firing squad himself in short order, Dmitry countered with what he thought logical. "If you wish Colonel, I can accomplish just that and be on my way."

Shtemenko stood and walked the few paces to where Dmitry stood at attention and sized up the man in front of him. Dirty, unshaven and disheveled, Lt. Abramenkov's bearing was still evident. Shtemenko offered a test. "That won't be necessary Lieutenant, as I have greater plans in mind for our good Germans. Indulge me, Dmitry Borisovich, why these civilians? What made them different and important enough to capture the attention of a tank commander?"

Shtemenko's choice to refer to Dmitry by his first and father's name, usually reserved for close friends, were not lost on Dmitry. Although weak of body, he was still sharp of mind, an ability he had developed for survival both from enemies abroad and from within. "Colonel, as you wish. The man was well fed and his hands were soft. Therefore, he was neither a farmer as he was dressed, nor a soldier. Yet, he was of solid body, and should be serving his country during its last dying gasp. The boy was old enough to be serving, and therefore, was either AWOL or exempt due to privilege. Although both the mother and daughter had made attempts to appear disheveled, their pampered existence and long grooming habits could ultimately not be concealed. So, either this man is a high ranking Nazi party official or a man of nobility. In either event, they were headed away from the front and Berlin, most likely in an attempt to flee the country or, at least, to the American lines."

"Very good, Dmitry Borisovich, I can see why your commanders saw fit to grant you a command at such a young age. And yes, you are right to a degree. This man and his family are not farmers, and yes, they are of privilege so to speak. The man's name is Wilhelm Bauer. He was a leading German scientist, most recently assigned to Peenemunde, where the Germans had produced much of their rocket technology. Bauer was chiefly responsible for the development of their V2 rocket, which brought much destruction upon our British friends," Shtemenko explained. Shtemenko's voice inflection when using the term "friends" was not loss on Dmitry. "So you see Comrade, you have caught quite a large fish. As a result, I forgive you for awakening me," Shtemenko added with a slight bit of whimsy in his voice.

Dmitry internalized a sigh of relief, not wanting to exhibit anything but complete control in front of the GRU officer. He also took pride, if only briefly, for trusting his instincts. Over the course of the past few years, he had developed a keen sense which had often saved him from one close battle to the next. "My men and I were only doing our duty for Mother Russia, nothing more, Colonel Shtemenko. If I may, dawn will be breaking soon and I should return to my tank and crew, as today's victories are impatient for my return."

"Dmitry Borisovich, yes, victories await, but from today forward, yours will not be fought on common battlefields. Instead, your destiny has been changed by today's events. Your future battles will be fought and won in different, less blunt ways. But these battles will shape the world's future in our favor. I'm reassigning you to my personal staff for the duration of what is left of this war, as your abilities and prospects will follow a more exclusive path. Inform your sergeant to return to what is now his crew, and see Captain Viktor Semenkov outside, for your work with our new German friends is not yet finished. Dismissed."

    And with his dismissal, Dmitry again sensed what must be likened to hope, his possible future.

Chapter 11
Atlantic Ocean
May 1945

Howard and Vincent Black's crew arrived at Gourock, Scotland by way of train and bus on a beautiful spring morning. The Aquitania, an old but stately four-stacker, and last of its kind operated by Cunard Luxury Lines, was docked and awaiting departure for New York. She was captained by the venerable George Gibbons. Earlier in the war, the Aquitania had been challenged by a U.S. reserve destroyer upon her arrival in New York. Gibbons, a salty seafarer remarked, "We are the only fuckin' four funnel ship in the world and that so-and-so wants are name! Go tell him to read the 'News of the World,'" which was followed by more colorful expletives.

The week spent aboard the Aquitania offered a full menu of experiences. Formerly deprived men were not for want, as they were now able to access booze, American cigarettes, hot meals, and showers. For the air crews who had access to such luxuries during their postings in the English countryside, these offerings were normal. However, for the soldier in the theatre and on the ground, living in cold, wet, and deplorable conditions, life aboard the Aquitania was living life at its best. Many expended their saved earnings on reckless card games and avoided soberness. Howard, outside of meals with Black and his crew, often sought the quiet tranquility on the upper deck in the early morning hours; contemplating his loss of Mae, and his return to sleepy Otho. Nevertheless, he felt hope stirring deep inside as he contemplated the possibilities for his future and adventures not yet realized.

"Your backside looks like it's healed well enough. How about the cobwebs in your head?" A somewhat familiar voice called from behind.

Howard turned to see Captain Jack Larsen standing tall with a drink in his hand, a fag hanging from his lips, and a slight mischievous smile fixed on his face. Before Howard could reply, Larsen continued with a wink, "Well, maybe the old noggin is still a bit fuzzy."

"No Sir," replied Howard, "I was just lost in thought. Wow, I'm surprised to run into you. I thought you would have already hit the states."

"Howard, again, call me Jack for Christ' sake. After all, at the end of the day, we are just two boys from Iowa. To answer your question, I stayed a bit longer than expected. But enough about me, how are you feeling?"

"Great Sir... Sorry, Jack. The doc cleared me for duty not too long after we met at the hospital. They told me all the results of the tests for lingering issues from the concussion were positive, and once I was on my feet and moving about, my leg muscles didn't take too long to rebound. I do have to admit my right cheek is still a bit sore, but I've learned to favor it when sitting or lying down," Howard said as he absently rubbed his backside. "I'm sure in good time that the scar tissue will loosen up and I'll be back to putting in a few rounds in the ring. When I got out, I made it back to Framlingham only to find that Hassig and my crew had already left for home. I ran into a fellow crew from the 570th, they took me on, and I shipped out with them soon after. I was really only back at the base long enough to say goodbye to a few old friends, and collect my back pay and property."

From further down the walkway, Black and Technical Sergeant Kyle Macmillan, better known to his friends as Mac, stood overlooking the ocean and the wake left by the Aquitania. "Say, Mac, isn't that Howard further down talking to some Captain?" asked Black.

"Sure thing, Lieutenant. I wonder how Howard would know a snake like that?" remarked Mac, with a bite to his tone.

"Not sure I follow you, Mac. How do you know that captain? It looks like he's from a different bomber group."

"Don't really know him, just know about him from what I've seen on board. He conned his way into a friendly game of poker some of the boys and I were having below decks, and then took a bundle from all of us. Not sure how he did it, but didn't look like luck to me or the rest of the boys. Later that night, I saw him horn his way between a Red Cross dame with great legs and a lieutenant, which looked to me like he had a great chance until the captain showed. When the lieutenant put up a fuss, that captain got in his face, pulled rank, and bullied him until he left dejected. Doesn't seem to me to be the kind of friend I would want."

Chapter 12
West of Berlin
May 12, 1945

Upon finding an American sergeant from the U.S. 44th Infantry Division, Wilhelm Bauer and his 15 year old son Johan approached the soldier, who was atop a bicycle, and called out in broken English. "My name is Wilhelm Bauer. I was part of the V-2 rocket program and I want to surrender."

Bauer and his son were delivered forthwith to Battalion Headquarters and interviewed by Captain Seamus O'Leary, the Division S-2 in charge of intelligence. During his interrogation by O'Leary, Bauer denied active involvement in the Nazi party, but admitted he had no choice but to join the party or face imprisonment and sequestration from his life's work.

When questioned about his motivation to surrender to American Forces, Bauer explained, "My team knows we have created the future of warfare, and the question as to what nation, to what victorious nation we are willing to entrust this brainchild of ours is a moral decision more than anything else. Many of us want to see the world spared another conflict, and I feel that surrendering such a weapon to people who are guided by democratic principles and a higher sense of morality could such assurances to the world be best secured."

Captain O'Malley was well aware of how important their catch was, as Bauer had been near the top of the American high command's Black List, the code name for the list of German scientists and engineers targeted for immediate interrogation by U.S. military experts. In June 1945, Bauer assisted O'Malley's team to locate others from his rocket research group. Once assembled, Bauer and the others were relocated to Munich. The group was later flown to Witzenhausen, a small town in the American Zone set up after the official end of the war in the European theatre. Bauer and the others were briefly detained at the "Dustbin" interrogation center at Kransberg Castle where the elite of the Third Reich's economy, science and technology were debriefed by U.S. and British intelligence officials. Eventually, Bauer was recruited by the U.S. under a program called "Operation Overcast," afterward known as "Operation Eagles Head."

Chapter 13
New York City
Mid-May, 1945

The news of the war's end in Europe was announced to the world on May 8th 1945, while Howard, Larsen, and Black were aboard the Aquitania transiting across the Atlantic. The old girl docked at Pier 54, one of a set known as Chelsea Piers running along the West Side of Manhattan. Immediately, New York City with all of its fanfare and overwhelming exuberance, was a stark contrast to the often reserved folk of England, and the mostly lazy and idyllic countryside in Suffolk. But the boys were ready.

The scene day and night in New York City was electric and without restraint. Restaurants, bars, and women were open 24 hours a day in one open-ended party. The atmosphere was intoxicating for a small town kid. Jack Larsen took the lead on all things, but Howard did not shy away from the allure of the big city and he took to it like a moth to a flame. Mid-way across the Atlantic, Jack learned of Howard's heart breaking letter from Mae and he did his best to help Howard move on. Jack was a talented womanizer, but he always made sure his target for the night had a girlfriend for Howard.

Over the period of a few crazy days, nightclubs, theatres, and late night diners became familiar friends to Howard. The war, with its constant threat of death aside, exposed Howard to outside cultures and customs. His new adopted family of airmen from all over the country, and now the energy of big city life changed Howard. In New York City, then and there, Howard knew he would not settle in Otho, or anywhere else in the Midwest. His life was meant to take a different, more adventurous path, full of meaning and impact.

Howard and Jack entered the Stage Door Canteen, a USO club on 44th Street, for one last night of revelry. Although all canteens were dry clubs, the Stage Door was wall to wall with returning soldiers, sailors, and airmen. But more importantly, the club was alive with young and readily available women. The music from the large piece band was loud and energetic, but what most captured Howard's attention was a young, very beautiful, auburn haired woman with firm legs and alluring bright green eyes. She was not dressed in the standard uniform of a USO hostess. From across the room, Howard could see many men of various ranks and service approach this angel, but reaction made it clear she was not available beyond a friendly smile and conversation. Howard took a chance and approached. Her name was Fran, short he learned for Francis. Although she was from the Clinton Hill neighborhood in Brooklyn, she had time for a small town kid from Iowa. As they talked and he looked into her mesmerizing eyes, for the first time, Howard knew he could move on from Mae.

Chapter 14
Des Moines, Iowa
May 1945

The party was intense but short lived in New York as Howard's furlough was up as soon as it began. Leaving the bright lights behind, Howard and Jack began what was to be a very long and convoluted journey back to Iowa, having to change trains in Buffalo, Chicago, and finally stopping in Des Moines at the Rock Island line station. Here, Howard and Jack split, promising to keep in touch.

"So where does life take you now, Howard?" Larsen probed as they pulled into the Des Moines rail station.

"I've made up my mind, especially after seeing New York. I'm going to submit my admissions application to Iowa State right away, using that GI Bill the Army promised would be waiting for me. I can't see myself back in Otho. Don't get me wrong, I love my folks, brother and sisters, but small time life and all of its trappings are not meant for me. I want to see the world, live life to its fullest, and if I can, make a difference," Howard exclaimed.

"How about you Jack? Are you returning to the police department in Waterloo? Going to stop chasing so many skirts and settle down?"

"Yes to the police department and no to the chasing part," Jack said with his disingenuous smile. "Prior to joining the Army Air Corps, I worked a fugitive case with a couple of FBI G-Men out of Minneapolis. They really impressed me with their polished manner, confidence, and tenacity. They knew I was heading off to flight training and told me to give them a call when I got back if I was interested in joining up. You know Howard, I don't think either one of us was meant to live out our lives here in small town U.S.A. Once I check in with my folks and the Chief, I'm making a call to the FBI office in Minneapolis about joining the big leagues. I'll send you a letter to let you know how it all goes. Leave your forwarding address with your folks so I can find you at the university." Jack took a quick look at his watch. "Well, better hurry over to the depot if I want to make the bus to Waterloo this afternoon," Jack said as he extended his hand to Howard. "Howard, follow your dreams and don't look back. Best of luck and keep in touch," Jack advised while smacking Howard's opposite shoulder with his free hand.

"Plan on it," Howard said with assuredness, "And same to you, Jack."

Both men picked up their life's belongings and turned to face their respective futures, not knowing then their lives would intersect again in due time.

Chapter 15
Otho, Iowa
May 1945

The bus arrived in Fort Dodge early in the morning. So early, not even the paperboys and milkmen were plying their trades. Much too early to call his folks for a ride, Howard threw his GI bag over his shoulder and started walking down Highway US 20 on a crisp, clear morning with the sun peeking over the horizon. It struck Howard that the countryside in Iowa was remarkably similar to England, although Iowa was a bit more flat. Howard thought about how his folks would react when they caught sight of him. It had been nearly two years since he last saw them on leave before heading to Sioux Falls. He thought it best he wait a bit before telling them he would be heading off to Iowa State University in Ames.

As Howard was lost in thought, an old Ford pick-up rattled to a stop beside him. Olaf Peterson reached across the bench seat and opened the passenger door as well as he could. "Howard, Howard Brooks, is that you?" bellowed the elderly Peterson with both a bit of surprise and glee in his voice. Mr. Peterson hadn't seen Howard in many years, and instead of a boy, a man now stood outside his passenger window.

"Mr. Peterson, well how do you do, sir? You're a great sight to see," Howard exclaimed.

"Howard, your parents will be overwhelmed to see you. How long have you been gone son?"

"Better part of two years, sir. I just arrived on the bus from Des Moines. I wrote the folks while on the transport ship coming home, but I don't know if they got my letter or not. Either way, they aren't expecting me this morning," Howard explained.

"Well, don't be so sure. Mothers have an uncanny sense when it comes to their children. Your mom has probably been baking a pie everyday waiting for you. Now get in Howard and throw your bag in the back amongst the bags of feed. How about Clarence, Howard? Any word on his return?"

"I'd be the last to know, I guess. Mom and Dad didn't send anything about Clarence's return in their last letter. But that has been a couple of months. Last I heard, he was aboard the USS Grimes transporting Marines somewhere in the Pacific. Just hope all is right in his world. I understand the Japanese have been giving us a hell of a time," Howard said as his voice trailed off in quiet reflection.

"Well, God was always with you two boys. Now, let's get you home and surprise your folks. Your dad won't be heading off to work for about an hour yet," Peterson remarked.

They covered the rest of the miles in silence as the sun continued to rise and shine brightly over the newly planted fields of Iowa gold. It was good to be home, even if it wouldn't be for long.

Chapter 16
The Brooks Household, Otho, Iowa
May 1945

As Howard said his thanks to Mr. Peterson and grabbed his bag from the back, he turned towards his home while placing his cover on top of his head. It was a habit really, not wanting to be caught out of uniform. Howard started up the front walk towards the porch, but froze at the sight of his mother Madge opening the front screen door to retrieve the morning's milk delivery. Howard didn't want to startle her and have his morning breakfast spilt all over the front porch. So instead, he waited until she walked back into the house and followed. Once inside, Howard quietly laid down his bag on the hallway carpet and tiptoed towards the kitchen and its smell of strong coffee and real eggs.

At the table, Howard's father William sat with a copy of the Fort Dodge Messenger and Chronicle spread wide and covering his face, a cup of steaming coffee off to his right. With his mother Madge's back to him as she prepared the morning spread, Howard announced, "Well, this is some kind of welcome home. I thought maybe a big band and a banner out front would be in order."

The sound of a breaking plate, followed by the fast ripple of newspaper, preceded a gasp from Madge and a grunt from William. "Oh my Lord, Howard! Howard my dear!" Madge exclaimed as she ran the few short paces separating them and wrapped her arms around Howard. As Howard's last breath was escaping his lungs, his father interceded.

"Now Mother, let the boy go so I can get a good look at him. Son, you look very fit and trim. Mother and I were worried sick after receiving your last letters from the hospital in England. We had no idea you had been released, let alone were returning home. How long are you home for, Howard? When do you ship out again?"

"Sorry about that, but with the move from the hospital and my return to the base, things moved so quickly. Before I knew it, I was being sent home. While in New York, the Army Air Force released me from service. I'm out Dad, my war is done."

"Thank God, son. We have much to catch up on, but why don't we just sit down at the table like the old days and share a home cooked breakfast made by your wonderful mother," William suggested.

They did just that, with Madge joining them, something she rarely did while Howard was a child. They discussed Howard's journey home and his injuries, touching only the surface of the Liberty Belle tragedy, and not even broaching his situation with Mae. Howard sensed they already knew about Mae. There would be time to talk about such things later, including Howard's future plans now that he was home.

Chapter 17
Moscow, Russia
Early June 1945

Lt. Dmitry Abramenkov's future was made for him. GRU Colonel Sergei Shtemenko had reassigned him to his staff, and Dmitry accompanied Shtemenko on the journey back to Moscow. Only two of the prisoners made the trip with them.

Upon arrival in Moscow, Dmitry was assigned immediately to the GRU training academy, known as the Military-Diplomacy of the General Staff of the Armed Forces (VDA), the beginning of his future with the intelligence apparatus. With his assignment, he lost contact with the prisoners and they soon faded from his memory, their fate no longer important.

At the ultra-secret intelligence academy, Dmitry's aptitude for languages earned him an assignment in the America's program, for which English language instruction was paramount. Dmitry flourished, impressing his instructors as he took to the fine art of tradecraft like a fish to water. Dmitry was a natural, adept at what they threw at him physically and psychologically. The latter issue was a bit of a challenge, as he was not born entirely from the training regiment, but more from the undercurrents of a political system. A system which was, by its very nature, suspicious of all, even its most devoted and ardent followers. All things considered, the three years passed by easily for Dmitry as he rarely met insurmountable obstacles from his academy instructors or the Party staff.

Chapter 18
Iowa State University
Ames, Iowa
July 1945

Howard broke the news to his parents about leaving for college, and the conversation had gone remarkably well, at least with his father. Although his mother was happy to see the first of her children seek a college education, their separation caused by war left her feeling cheated. Most troubling, she knew he wasn't coming back and that she had lost her baby to the world. William, on the other hand, understood a man's need to strike out on his own and fulfill his own fate. He was, of course sad, for Mother.

Howard decided to start classes immediately and not wait for the fall. Not knowing exactly where he was headed, Howard first majored in business, but quickly changed to engineering. Howard's years spent listening to his wireless, and his experiences as a radio operator, drew him in that logical direction. He felt a burning sense of urgency for his future, making up for years lost to war and living only day to day. Howard took his courses seriously and avoided outside distractions, including love. He had clearly moved on from Mae, but was in no mood to repeat love gained and love lost. Howard didn't want anything to stand between himself and destiny.

Chapter 19
New York Office of the FBI
New York City
June 1948

Jack Larsen, Special Agent of the FBI, picked up the phone receiver and announced, "Larsen."

"Jack, it's Joan. I have a Howard Brooks on the line, said he knows you from the 8th Air Force." Announced Joan, one of five switchboard operators assigned to the New York Office of the FBI.

"Outstanding Joan, put him through please," Jack requested, happy to take the call. "Howard, you there?"

"Jack, is it okay for you to take a call at work?" Howard asked, not sure whether or not he was causing problems for the G-man.

"Damn straight it is Howard," Jack answered with enthusiasm. "I'll take a call from an old Air Force buddy and fellow Iowegan any day. How are you Howard? And where are you calling from?"

"I'm calling from the Otho Mercantile store, Jack. My parents still don't have a phone installed. Mom thinks such things are frivolous."

"Big word from a small town kid," Jack jested. "What has it been, about a year I guess since we last talked, right? Did you finish your degree at Iowa State?"

"Just did Jack, and thought I would give you a call and maybe come out and visit New York while I still sort through a few things," Howard expressed. "Still have a couch I can crash on for a day or two?" Howard asked with a bit of hesitation, not wanting to impose on Jack and his meandering ways.

"Absolutely Howard, you can call on old Jack anytime. And if you're coming all the way to New York, plan on staying for more than a day or two. When were you thinking about coming to town?"

"Well, now actually. I need a break after fast tracking my degree and before I start looking for a job. I've had two offers already, both at agricultural science companies in Des Moines, but I'm not sure about either. I need a distraction to clear my mind a bit, and couldn't think about a better way than a train ride to New York City and a few nights out with the legendary Jack Larsen," Howard joked, only half heartedly because Jack was somewhat of a legend to Howard.

"Well Howard, that sounds like a plan. If you've got a pen and paper, I'll give you my address. When you get in, go there straight away and see my landlady Mrs. Voronova. I'll leave word to let you in. I usually call it a day about 1800 and should be home soon after. Help yourself to any cold cuts and beer in the fridge, Howard. It will sure be great to see an old friend," Jack exclaimed with meaning in his voice.

"That's great Jack, look forward to it. Take care and I'll see you soon," Howard replied with a bit of relief. He was happy to know Jack would be so welcoming.

Howard placed the receiver back on the hook, and took a good look around. The place was quiet, too quiet.

Chapter 20
GRU Headquarters
Moscow
July 1948

Dmitry stood at attention in front of General Shtemenko's desk, having being summoned the day after graduation from the VDA. Dmitry eagerly awaited his first assignment. He hoped for one abroad. Having mastered English, his assignments would logically take him to the West. But he also understood he had no say in such matters. His fate lied in the hands of the GRU and Soviet party machine, both of which often defied logic. On the plus side, he had met Tatiana the year before. She was beautiful, kind, and intelligent. All traits Dmitry had found lacking in many of the girls he had allowed to come into his life, all leaving by his own accord. His Tatiana was different, and he hoped to marry her now that he was finished with the academy. He hoped she would say yes, and they could start a family together.

"Dmitry Borisovich, at ease and take a seat," Shtemenko ordered with the tinge of a fatherly tone. "You have done well, exceptionally well, Dmitry. Your country is proud. I am proud. Your father would be also if here today," Shtemenko added with fervor. "I have plans for you Dmitry Borisovich, many plans. I'm arranging to have you assigned to our official Consulate in New York. You will use the cover of Vice-Consul. This cover title and the centralized location of the Consulate on East 61st Street will afford you much freedom of movement and logical access. However, Dmitry, you will not immediately report to this assignment. Over the next two years, I will be providing you with some additional and specialized training, training reserved only for you, Dmitry. But first, let's see about your marriage to your lovely Tanya."

Dmitry was not surprised the GRU knew of Tatiana, after all, he had to report his contacts with her. But Shtemenko's knowledge of his intentions for marriage took him a bit by surprise. A lesson he must remember as he navigated the rest of his career and life.

Chapter 21
Chelsea Neighborhood
New York City
July 1948

Howard arrived midday by train at Grand Central Station. It was as he remembered, overcrowded with men, women, and children heading in a hundred different directions. But missing were the men in uniform, a good thing, Howard thought, a nation finally at peace. It was a beautiful day as Howard emerged from the station with his small bag in tote. He decided to walk since he had a couple of hours to kill before Jack would be home. He chose Broadway Avenue because of his fond memories from some three years prior. Mid-year 1945 was a very joyous time for Howard, along with the thousands of other men returning from war. But for Howard, the area near the theatre district held even fonder memories. He had met Fran at the Stage Door Canteen, the only woman to captivate Howard's attention since Mae. The only woman he had allowed himself to think about since.

Howard arrived in front of Jack's apartment building, an old tenement structure from the area's formally prominent Scottish population. Upon entering the front hall, he was met by an elderly woman. Oddly enough, she called to him using his first name. But then Howard remembered he was to ask for Mrs. Voronova. She escorted Howard to Jack's apartment on the ground floor. As she opened the door, Howard caught a glimpse of a beautiful young woman exiting an apartment a few doors down. She had long blonde flowing hair and a very snug skirt and blouse. As Howard turned back towards the apartment door to enter, he noticed a scowl affixed across Mrs. Voronova's face. Inside, Howard stowed his bag in a small hall closet and surveyed his surroundings. Jack had taste. Although a pre-war building, Jack had added some modern and masculine touches including an art deco styled bar displaying various liquor bottles and cocktail bar ware. Howard opened the small refrigerator door and grabbed a Rheingold bottled beer. The cold and light elixir was just what he needed to shake the effects of a long train trip across the country. After finishing the better part of a second lager, Howard rested his head on the back of a stylish yet comfortable leather chair, and closed his eyes with a smile on his face. A man could get used to this, Howard thought.

Howard awoke at the sound of the apartment door opening. In walked Jack, an FBI standard issued fedora in his hand.

"Howard, old buddy! When I told you to make yourself at home, you really took me seriously!" Jack exclaimed with bravado as his hand swept from side to side at the sight of the empty bottles of beer. "Couldn't wait for the appropriate cocktail hour, I guess?"

"It was a long, long train ride Jack," Howard replied with a smile on his face. Howard rose to shake Jack's hand, but Jack caught him mid stride and gave him a big bear hug.

"Great to see you, old friend. I've been really looking forward to your visit after all these years. Go ahead and sit back down while I grab a cold one. You want another?" Jack asked as he walked the few feet to the small galley kitchen open to the living room.

"I'll just hold off a bit until I get something in my stomach if you don't mind. And it's great to see you too Jack. I hoofed it all the way down from Grand Central to take in the sights. Sure brought back a bunch of good memories," Howard remarked.

"Yes, the city in the spring is beautiful isn't it, especially with the pavement full of young women sans long coats and scarves?" Jack said as a matter of fact. "Just think of us back in 1945, Howard. We had survived and come back to a world of possibilities. And just look at us now," Jack replied with true enthusiasm in his voice. "Two relatively young and definitely handsome guys without a care in the world. How about we get cleaned up and hit the town? I've got a few new places to show you," Jack offered with a grin on his face as he removed his suit jacket exposing a Colt .45 hanging from a shoulder holster. "But first, we need to buy you a proper hat," Jack said as he donned his fedora.

During a quiet dinner at Angelo's of Mulberry Street in the heart of Little Italy, Howard and Jack got caught up on the missing years since their first foray in the city, after returning from England in spiffy uniforms with back pay in their pockets. Jack asked most of the questions, with Howard filling in the details about college, his folks back in Iowa, and info on boys form Howard's bomber group. As Jack asked question after question over plates of antipasto and glasses of house wine, Howard sensed Jack was relatively happy and content with his work for the FBI. But Howard sensed something he couldn't quite put his finger on. Perhaps Jack was a bit lonely, with the years of carousing and bachelorhood catching up with him. Or maybe isolation in the big city away from family and friends had taken their toll. Whatever it was, Howard sensed a barely perceivable undercurrent of something that caused Jack to lose a bit of his carefree and maverick self. But in the end, Howard marked it up to Jack's years on the job, first as a police detective and now as an FBI agent.

"Well Howard," Jack started while refilling each of their wine glasses, "So what's your plan from here? Are you really looking forward to applying your engineering degree and staying in Iowa?"

"That would be the sensible thing to do I guess, but it just doesn't feel right, you know. I've always believed in fate, destiny, God's plan, whatever you want to call it. Joining the Army and signing up for heavy bombers just felt right. I never gave it a second thought. It was the same thing with leaving Otho and heading off to college, really. Don't get me wrong, the offers I received have been great, and I really couldn't go wrong choosing either of the leading candidates. It's just…" Howard paused, searching for the right words.

"Howard, you and I are very similar that way," Jack interrupted. "You just know when you know. Take me for example, policing has always been in my blood I believe, and after meeting those two agents out of Minneapolis, I just knew the FBI was right for me. Say Howard, I want you to give some thought to an alternative to directly applying your degree in private industry. The Bureau predominantly hires lawyers and accountants, but your keen and analytical mind would make you very competitive. Have you ever given thought to a career in the FBI?" Jack asked with enthusiasm in his voice.

It was at this moment that things all started to come together for Howard. Jack's broaching of the idea of pursuing a career in the FBI just made sense. Jack's stories, although vague at best, were full of intrigue and purpose. Howard had been on a continual search for adventure and a way out of small town Iowa. Working for the FBI could definitely satisfy both. "Jack, you've been at this game for a while now, be honest with me, do I have what it takes?"

"I wouldn't have brought it up if I didn't, Howard. I also suspected that your trip here was for a purpose. You may not believe it, but I think you and I were meant to meet and become friends. Destiny or whatever you want to call it. Howard, the war we fought in the skies, on the ground, and upon the sea, ended because men like you and I were not afraid to go into harm's way. But Howard, a new threat has emerged, maybe even more sinister than Hitler and war hungry Japan. The Soviet Union and their Godless Communism is our new threat. The work we do in New York is key to countering this threat. We could use a good man like you, Howard. Just say the word, and I'll make arrangements to introduce you to my supervisor in the office.

Howard didn't have to dwell on the offer. By the time he put his half-full glass of wine down, he had made up his mind. Howard and Jack spent the night going from one joint to the next as Jack played tour director. All along, Howard sensed an inner peace, built on knowing he had found his calling and his future was on track. Howard looked forward to calling the Bureau his home.

Chapter 22
FBIHQ, Washington DC
November 1948

Three years after leaving the FBI's New York Office for FBIHQ, Supervisor Robert J. Lamphere had developed a reputation in the Counterespionage section of the Bureau's Security Division as a detailed and tenacious agent. In late 1947, he met for the first time with Meredith Knox Gardner, a brilliant Army Security Agency cryptanalyst and linguist who was working on deciphering the Soviet wartime communications codes. The operation was codenamed Verona. Gardner's painstaking work was aided by the charred remnants of a Soviet code book found on a battlefield in Finland in 1944, as well as intercepted coded Soviet intelligence messages.

Lamphere had offered to provide Gardner with information that the FBI might have, or be able to obtain, regarding a particular subject being discussed in one of the deciphered message fragments. As a result of information supplied by the FBI, Gardner began making slow but steady progress in breaking the code. Such breaks led to the deciphering of Soviet messages sent between Moscow and their New York intelligence referentura, the Soviets' secure accommodation inside its diplomatic premises; reserved for the exclusive use of intelligence personnel, including an office for the Resident, a cipher room, and a soundproof vault in which conversations can be conducted without fear of eavesdropping.

Included in the decoded messages were cover names assigned to Soviet intelligence officers assigned in New York, their agents, organizations, people, or places of interest. Not possessing further identifiable information, such cover names would only serve the collective knowledge of the FBI. More alarming were the decrypts of cover names assigned to GRU agents. Among these were KORN, MORSE, and BRAVE, all possible active agents run by the GRU in the United States.

Chapter 23
New York City
May 1950

Howard had entered the FBI training program split between the Old Post Office Pavilion on Pennsylvania Avenue at 11th Street in downtown Washington, DC and the Marine base at Quantico, Virginia in the early spring of 1949. He experienced no problems with the rigorous entrance exams and personal scrutiny, having received a personal recommendation from Jack Larsen's superiors. The training itself was demanding, both physically and academically; but Howard enjoyed the challenge and thrived in the setting, quickly earning a reputation as having a calm demeanor and a gift for interrogation. His instructors attributed his communication skills to growing up in rural Iowa with its friendly sensibilities and dependence on personal interaction and cooperation necessary for survival in a small community. His time spent operating the Army radio set helped Howard hone his attention to detail, and he innately possessed an inquisitive mind. Classes were held in all investigative disciplines, including instruction on the Soviet intelligence apparatus, as well as the intelligence agencies of "friendly" countries. The academy staff detailed successful investigations and arrests of German and Soviet saboteurs and spies, including many by the New York Office. These included the 1941 arrest of German spy Frederick Joubert "Fritz" Duquesne and several others in his spy ring who provided secret information on Allied weaponry and shipping movements to William Sebold, a confidential FBI informant; and the 1942 arrest of German saboteurs led by George John

Dasch, who had landed by U-boat on a beach near Amagansett, Long Island, New York. Dasch turned himself in at the New York Office two days after landing. Within two weeks, the FBI captured all 8 saboteurs. In 1948, a New York grand jury indicted former State Department employee Alger Hiss for perjury. The charge stemmed from a congressional investigation of Communist subversion and espionage in the government.

Howard also enjoyed the "bull in the ring" boxing, his first foray back in the ring after competing in Golden Gloves matches in Fort Dodge. Not being much of a bruiser, Howard was a tactical boxer, using his head to apply strategy and not as a punching bag.

Upon graduation, Howard was sent directly to the New York Office, unlike most new agents who were sent to serve in smaller offices, as far away from their upbringing as possible to learn the finer points of the FBI system. As much as Howard had enjoyed his FBI training, with its classes on foreign espionage and his acquired knowledge of FBI successes in New York, investigating Nazi and Soviet spies, he longed to get started on his assignment with Jack in New York.

Howard exited Penn Station and surfaced on 33rd Street, having arrived by an early morning train. It was a rainy and unseasonably cool Saturday; but Howard didn't mind, he was excited to get on with his career and work together with Jack. Howard donned his Fedora as a proper FBI Agent, and as he looked about, he felt a stab in his lower back as a man's voice commanded, "Don't move or I'll shoot." Howard's training prepared him to act immediately, and as he stepped to his left and started to pivot, his left hand came up in a blocking motion to meet his attacker's arm. By instinct, Howard started to bring his right arm up in a powerful jab intended to strike his attacker under the bridge of his nose. But something caused Howard to slow his punch in mid form. It was Jack's face wearing a "cat caught the canary" grin.

"Glad to see all that training paid off, Agent Brooks," Jack said trying hard to conceal a chuckle building in his throat.

"You're just lucky I decided not to take a free shot," Howard replied as a smile built across his face and he noticed Jack holding his right hand with extended index finger and upright thumb in the form of a gun.

"How was the trip, old man? Meet any lovely ladies on the ride up?"

"None that I would tell you about, Mr. Casanova, for fear you would try to worm your way in. So, how about grabbing one of these bags for your "old friend?" Howard asked, not waiting for an answer as he passed off one of his hard side cases to Jack.

"Sure old man. Let's hail a cab and drop your bags off at my place on the way to the office. SAC Williams is expecting his newest tool in the box," Jack replied as he stepped towards the curb with his arm extended.

The cab dropped them off in front of a well kept apartment building in Greenwich Village, to the east of Washington Square campus of New York University (NYU). Jack walked them up the third floor and opened the door for Howard. Howard was amazed by the spaciousness. Jack had clearly moved up in the world during the last couple of years.

In fact, Jack walked Howard down a short hall to an extra bedroom. "Well, home sweet home, old man," Jack announced dropping Howard's bag and spreading his arms wide.

"Wow," was all that Howard could muster; clearly impressed by the place he would call home until he could get settled. "Jack, this is more than I expected, way more."

"Well, you know Howard, a single and handsome man like me has to impress the ladies. You are welcome to stay as long as you need. After all, two old flyboys from Iowa are more like family than anything else," Jack added with a touch of sincerity Howard was not accustomed to seeing from him. "No time to dawdle, old man. The real 'Old Man' is waiting," Jack announced referring to SAC Williams.

Chapter 24
Picatinny Arsenal
September 1950

After spending nearly three years at Fort Bliss in El Paso, Texas, Wilhelm Bauer was looking forward to a change. His son Johan had done well in school, finishing near the top of his class. A small wonder Wilhelm thought, even though expectations were high from the son of an accomplished rocket scientist, the fate of Johan's mother and sister weighed heavily on their hearts and souls. They had somehow managed to put both in the deep recesses of their minds, but in doing so, a small bit of intimacy was lost between Wilhelm and his son. Deep down, Wilhelm knew Johan blamed him for whatever ungodly fate had befallen the two.

In June 1945, Bauer and others from the Peenemunde staff, ran by Wernher von Braun, had been brought to the U.S. as part of Operation Paperclip. Bauer was among those scientists for whom the U.S. Joint Intelligence Objectives Agency created false employment histories, and expunged Nazi Party memberships and regime affiliations from the public record. Once "bleached" of their Nazism, the U.S. Government granted the scientists security clearances to work in the United States.

While at Fort Bliss, Bauer helped train military, industrial, and university personnel in the intricacies of rockets and guided missiles. As part of the Hermes project, they helped refurbish, assemble, and launch a number of V-2s that had been shipped from Germany to the White Sands Proving

Grounds in New Mexico. They also continued to study the future potential of rockets for military and research applications.

In 1950, at the start of the Korean War, von Braun and most of his team were transferred to Huntsville, Alabama, where von Braun led the U.S. Army's rocket development team at the Redstone Arsenal. However, Bauer was reassigned to the Picatinny Arsenal as part of the Army's rocket and missile testing program, part of the broader U.S. response to a perceived Soviet threat following World War II. This helped place Picatinny in line for much R&D funding in nuclear weapons research. In 1949, Picatinny received its first nuclear assignment for a 280-millimeter atomic shell capable of being fired from a conventional artillery gun. The shell was nicknamed "Atomic Annie."

Bauer knew leaving Fort Bliss and relocating to New Jersey would be a refreshing move for Johan and himself. With the move came new freedoms as they would no longer feel locked down by the constraints of living on base under the constant watch of U.S. officials and fellow German scientists. They would be able to live in a quiet small town, and Johan could attend one of New Jersey's or New York's leading universities. However, Bauer also knew that the move would bring a series of more pressing and dangerous concerns. His only solace would be the thread of a hope that his wife and daughter would not be harmed.

Chapter 25
New York Office of the FBI
October 7, 1950

Howard had taken to the city like a fish to water. He quickly embraced all its idiosyncrasies, got used to the rat cage syndrome caused by too many people crammed into very tight spaces, and learned to ignore the potpourri of smells emanating from days' old garbage and steamy sewers. Howard had also learned how to navigate the FBI office environment where sitting at one's desk was seen as goofing off, and taking off your suit coat in the stifling summer heat was considered out of uniform. By order of Director Hoover, Agents had to track their time cards by codes representing the variety of work they performed. Most notably, the Time in Office (TIO) code was closely watched. If an Agent spent too much time in the office instead of on the street, they were graded poorly in performance reports. In reality, TIO caused many Agents to find creative ways to avoid office time. Long static surveillances on secondary targets and afternoons spent at the movie house often resulted. But Howard had spent years in the military, and the paramilitary nature of the FBI was somehow welcoming.

Howard's interview with SAC Williams, upon his arrival in May, had gone well. Williams had lectured Howard on the priorities of the office, and more specifically, his assignment working counterespionage. "Agent Brooks, counterespionage work in this office is a top priority. We may have won the last war against the German and Japanese menace, but our current war is just as threatening to our way of life and prosperity.

Make no mistake. Our 'allies' the Soviets are not our 'friends,' they are our foe. The Red Menace and its godless Communist system is the greatest threat known to our existence as a democratic system. The spread of Communism threatens every man, woman, and child in our great nation. Soviet spies are intent on infiltrating our government at every level, and our communities, no matter how large or small. Your job, Agent Brooks, is to toil tirelessly to stop the spread of this disease and to lop off its head. Welcome to the rolls of history Agent Brooks, welcome to the Cold War. You are now a spy catcher," Williams extolled.

After Howard's initial meeting with Williams, Jack had shown him to their squad area within the FBI office at 290 Broadway, New York, NY. Howard shared a desk space with Jack and theirs sat face to face with another shared by two other agents. One phone was shared by all with an outside line only obtained through the switchboard operator. Jack was not Howard's official training agent, a senior agent assigned to a junior agent with the responsibility of providing training not only on the program, but on the do's and don'ts of the office. Rather, Jack was Howard's de facto partner. Howard was the perfect student, understanding that the development of his administrative navigational skills was equally as important as the counterespionage and investigative training.

Howard walked out the front of their FBI office and set out for their assigned car, parked down the block on Thomas Street. Jack was a few minutes behind, stopping to notify the duty agent of the addresses they were heading to conduct verification checks for suspected Communist Party members. The Alien Registration Act, also known as the Smith Act, enacted in 1940, set criminal penalties for advocating the overthrow of the U.S. government, and required all non-citizen adult residents to register with the government. In 1949, after a ten-month trial at the Foley Square Courthouse in Manhattan, eleven leaders of the Communist Party were convicted under the Smith Act. Ten defendants each received a sentence of five years plus fines. Following that decision, the Department of Justice prosecuted dozens of cases. In addition to the Smith Act, the Internal Security Act of 1950, also known as the Subversive Activities Control Act or the McCarran Act, after its principal sponsor, was enacted over President Harry Truman's veto. The Act required Communist organizations to register with the United States Attorney General. It also established the Subversive Activities Control Board to investigate persons suspected of engaging in subversive activities, or otherwise promoting the establishment of a "totalitarian dictatorship," either Fascist or Communist. Members of these groups could not become citizens, and in some cases, were prevented from entering or leaving the country. Citizens found in violation could lose their citizenship in five years. The Act also contained an emergency detention statute, giving the President the authority to apprehend and detain "each person as to whom there is a reasonable ground to believe that such person probably will engage in, or probably will conspire with others to engage in, acts of espionage or sabotage."

    Howard pulled the car to the curb and slid over for Jack to drive. Howard was still learning to navigate the maze of streets in lower Brooklyn. After crossing the Brooklyn Bridge, they headed east on Flatbush Avenue to Ocean Avenue, heading towards Brighton Beach. Brighton Beach was largely occupied by ethnic Russian and Ukrainian immigrants and dubbed "Little Odessa" by the locals. Howard and Jack were searching for Alexander Mikailovich Zhukov, a chief member of a Communist worker's organization centered in Baltimore. Zhukov had fled the Baltimore area before agents in the Washington Field Office could execute an arrest warrant. SAC Williams had assigned Howard and Jack to check several addresses in the Brighton area known to be frequented by suspected members of the local New York chapter of the Communist Party USA (CPUSA). Neither Howard nor Jack believed the leads would lead anywhere, as the close knit community of Russian expats was not known for its cooperative nature. As Jack pulled the car to the curb, Howard could see the pedestrians on the sidewalk flanking Brighton Beach Avenue, shadowed by the elevated train tracks, glance their way, suspicious of outsiders. Howard's and Jack's senses were on full alert, as assistance from fellow agents or the local police this far out would be a long time coming.

"Howard, let me take the lead on this. I've been out here a few times on similar checks. Whatever you do, don't let anyone try to separate us," Jack whispered as they slowly exited the car, ensuring the holsters were readily available under their dark suits.

The lead from Washington indicated Zhukov may be staying with a distant cousin, whose elderly parents ran a butcher shop on the ground level of a three story building, with their residence occupying the second and third floors. Jack led the way through the open front door as his senses were assaulted by the strong acrid smell given off by the various meats hanging from hooks from the ceiling. Their approach was immediately met by a man in his late 60's, wearing a blood stained apron and having grey bushy eyebrows as impressive as the waves of thick hair slicked back across his rather large forehead. They were greeted by what could only be characterized as a semi-hostile exchange. "What do you want with us? Why have you come into my store? You have no business here," the elderly but yet stocky and confident man demanded.

"Where is Alexander Zhukov and your son Sergey Yakushev?" Jack retorted in an equally assertive tone, not offering his name and credentials with the FBI, as the elderly Yakushev was clearly aware they were Feds.

"You have no business with my son. He is a good boy and a hard worker. He is not here, now go away," Yakushev announced. Howard immediately recognized the way Yakushev had failed to deny even knowing Zhukov, let alone his whereabouts. As Jack began to reply with a now more aggressive tone, Howard sensed movement behind the elderly Yakushev, coming from a stockroom area accessed through a doorway behind the service counter. Trusting his instincts, Howard immediately made for the doorway. As the elderly Yakushev started his move to block Howard, Jack stiff armed Yakushev and followed immediately on the heels of Howard. Pushing through the curtain hanging from the doorway, Howard caught a glimpse of two subjects making a fast exit through a back door off to their right. Howard closed fast, and as he exited into the semi-shadows of a narrow alleyway lying between the back of Yakushev's store and an adjacent similar brick building, the two male subjects exited the alleyway and turned right. Howard turned the corner onto the sidewalk in a wide arc, anticipating trouble. And trouble was there in the form of a younger version of the elderly Yakushev, smack in the middle of launching his body to block their pursuers' exit.

Howard would have none of it. He planted both feet in a wide stance and grabbed the leading arm of the younger Yakushev, causing Yakushev to lose his balance. In a blur of movement, Howard drove his right knee into Yakushev's midsection receiving a loud grunt in exchange. As he began to apply an arm bar and take Yakushev down to the pavement, Jack rounded the corner, drew his handcuffs from the small of his back, applied a knee to the small of Yakushev's back, and applied the other to the back of Yakushev's neck. At the same time, Jack yelled for Howard to continue the pursuit of the second subject, assumed to be Zhukov, who now had a 30-40 foot lead on them both.

Howard didn't pause to argue, but instead, resumed his pursuit, building to an all out run. Howard was in great shape, having continued his regiment of running, sparring, and calisthenics at a local downtown gym frequented by New York City Police officers assigned to the 1st Precinct. Although quickly gaining on Zhukov, street obstacles including pedestrians, shopkeepers and open access doors in the sidewalk, stymied his efforts. With Jack out of play, Howard knew he had to finish on his own. And with that, he dug deep, bird dogged his prey, and finished the race with a leaping dive that resulted in Zhukov's very personal meeting with a parked Ford delivery truck. The blow stunned Zhukov and knocked the fight out of him. Howard claimed his prize in what he hoped would be his first of many arrests in New York.

Chapter 26
New York Office of the FBI
Same Day

With Yakushev already locked up, Howard and Jack went to work on Zhukov in an office holding room. Zhukov had regained his senses, but not his cooperative attitude. Although he was not shy in extolling the virtues of Communism; after all, in his own mind he was an expert, having lived under both the Soviet Communist system and America's democratic "dictatorship," Zhukov was resistant to identifying his associates in New York and Baltimore. Zhukov also readily acknowledged his CPUSA membership, a confession that would seal his fate. However, Howard and Jack wanted names, especially of CPUSA New York chapter members. The more pressure and "bad cop" posturing Jack applied, the more Zhukov detailed his ideology and the future of Communist rule in America. Howard remained quiet, studying Zhukov's body language and searching for a vulnerability he could exploit. After a couple of hours, Howard motioned for Jack to take a break and they stepped out of the room. While sipping piping hot coffee from white China mugs, Howard asked Jack to go out on a limb and allow him to interrogate Zhukov for a few minutes on his own. Not wanting to insult his friend Jack, Howard suggested that Jack had sufficiently softened Zhukov for the kill, but as a matter of Russian pride, he would have a hard time cooperating with Jack still in the room. Howard knew from his studies that Russians had carried a chip on their shoulder for hundreds of years, and breaking through was nearly impossible.

Howard re-entered the room, offering Zhukov a cup of coffee. Zhukov accepted, albeit reluctantly and suspicious of Howard's intentions. "Alexander, you are obviously a man of convictions. Although I don't agree with your ideology, I can respect a man who stands by his convictions," Howard started, noticing a slight relaxing in Zhukov's shoulders. "What I don't understand is how on one hand, men such as yourself, who are willing to risk all for their ideology, conceal the very things they should be most proud of."

"What do you mean by these things?" Zhukov replied with a suspicious tone.

"Alexander, my father taught me that a man is known by the company he keeps. That a man is judged by his friends and the organizations to which he belongs, because a man freely chooses these things, unlike a schoolboy whose friends are chosen by his mother. You are a man, are you not Alexander?" Howard asked, but not waiting for a reply. Howard understood that allowing a suspect to talk too early would allow him to form an immediate rebuttal, most likely a lie, a lie of which could become a psychological roadblock to a later confession. "You are obviously a proud man, Alexander. So you should be proud of your friends, your comrades in your shared struggle. Let them answer for themselves, for their ideology, as you are today. Let them demonstrate their own pride. How about it, Alexander? Your cooperation with me today is nothing more than an opportunity for you to further your cause, to voice your struggle. Who are your contacts in the New York CPUSA, Alexander? Who is it you are most proud to call your friends, who struggle with you in your glorious cause? Who Alexander? Who is it amongst your group that can best explain your struggle, your aspirations?

Name them Alexander, and I will personally see that they get their chance to argue the virtues of Communism," Howard finished with a crescendo of a preacher delivering a God-inspired sermon that he had been toiling over for six long days.

Alexander let go like a man who had held onto a secret far too long, a secret that had eaten at his very soul for years. And afterwards, he was spent, exhausted by the very release. Howard had names, many names, a list of local Communist Party members and sympathizers. Where this list would take the FBI, Howard could not know at the time. He hoped among amongst the names was the one true threat. The FBI had been searching for agents of the Soviet intelligence apparatus, U.S. citizens who had moved beyond ideology, who had crossed the line. Howard could only hope Alexander's list contained such a lead.

Chapter 27
New York City
October 10, 1950

For the second time in the week, Howard tackled another human being, only this time, it wasn't intentional. Howard walked out the front door of Jack's apartment building into an overcast, but relatively warm Saturday morning. He was wearing sweats and sneakers as he was about to set out on a mid-morning run. Although he was very grateful for Jack allowing him to sublet a room in his apartment, Howard enjoyed these times of solitude. He set off at a slow pace, allowing his muscles and lungs to warm up a bit before hitting his stride. Before long, he was entering the outskirts of the NYU campus and beginning to build momentum. Howard ran under the massive marble archway leading into Washington Square Park. The arch was modeled after the Arc de Triumph in Paris and built to mark the centennial of President George Washington's inauguration.

As Howard turned left on one of the many pebble stone pathways towards a large expanse of grass and open air, his right arm caught the torso of a woman heading in the opposite direction. The contact barely broke Howard's stride, but as he looked back over his shoulder to identify what he had hit, he saw arms and legs flailing and books flying. Howard stopped and turned back to offer a hand to help her off the ground, immediately noticing a look of menace on her face and sensing he was going to get an earful.

"Get your hands off me!" she demanded in a surprisingly forceful voice. "Who the heck do you think you are, flying about the campus without looking where you're going? You could have killed someone," she said with vitriol. Running out of steam and nasty rebukes, she paused for the first time and noticed Howard staring into her eyes with a smile forming on his face. "And what are you looking at?" she demanded.

What Howard was looking at was a dream, a most beautiful dream. Her auburn hair was a bit shorter, but still flowed like the waves rolling onto a magnificent beach at sunset. Her eyes were still a vibrant and captivating green. She had barely changed in the past five years.

"Francis, it's me Howard, Howard Brooks. We met at the Stagedoor back in '45 as I was passing through New York on my way back home to Iowa. Here, please let me help you up," he said as he again extended his hand. "I'm so sorry, and you're right, I should have been paying more attention to where I was going," Howard offered as Fran finally took his hand and rose to her feet.

As Fran used her hands to re-tuck the tail of her white blouse, smooth her skirt, and dust off her rear-end, she stared back into Howard's eyes. Howard noticed recognition quickly forming and a softening in her expression. "Technical Sergeant Howard Brooks from Otho, Iowa? A B-17 Radio Operator, right?" Fran said in the form of a statement more than a question. "I, I... What are you doing here, in New York?" she stammered.

Howard thought this to be a good, no, a very good sign. Fran not only remembered his name, but remembered quite a bit of detail from their brief time together so long ago. "Well, I live and work here now," Howard advised.

"On campus, here at New York University?" Fran asked with a look of confusion on her face.

"No, I'm sorry. I live nearby, just down the street. I'm out for a morning run," Howard said stating the obvious. "What are you doing here, here at NYU?" Howard asked as he bent to pick up an armful of books he had knocked from Fran's arms.

"I work here, Howard. When I met you, I was nearly finished with my Master's degree in physics and attending classes at the Polytechnic Institute in Brooklyn. Now, I'm teaching undergraduate physics courses at Washington Square College, which is NYU's Liberal Arts and Science College. I'm also helping with the Physics Department's transition back to this campus while I finish my graduate studies. In fact, I'm just now headed to our physics office. I can't believe you live and work here now. What is it you do, Howard?" Fran asked having now recovered her senses.

"Well, there have been a lot of changes in my life since returning from the war and having the great pleasure of meeting you," Howard said in a flirtatious tone. "Why don't I take you to dinner tonight so we can catch up?"

"I'm sorry Howard, but I'm busy tonight," Fran replied. With these words, Howard was disappointed, realizing Fran may not be as interested in him as he was in her. Or even worse, she was already taken, he thought, while trying to get a glimpse of her ring finger which was obscured by a pile of books she now held again.

Being the gentlemen he was, Howard decided to pull back and give her the room she obviously wanted. "Well, that's okay. It was nice running into you, both literally and figuratively. And it is good to learn you are doing so well," Howard said with a slight pause before continuing. "I'd better let you get on your way. I've got to cover a few miles myself. Take care Fran," Howard said as he started to move pass Fran and plot his route.

"Wait Howard," Fran asserted using the same tone as when she admonished him after being knocked to the ground. "I didn't say anything about not having dinner with you another time, did I? I'm just busy tonight as I'm attending a lecture on nuclear theory and a University cocktail reception that follows," Fran explained, her words stopping Howard in his tracks. Howard turned back towards Fran as hope reemerged. "You know Howard, I can bring a guest. Are you interested?" Fran asked with a devious smile forming on her lips.

Not in physics so much, Howard thought, but in you, yes, as a smile built on his face. "Fran, I would be delighted to be your guest," Howard replied as he closed the distance between the two. And as students, out for an early morning walk or heading to classroom buildings passed by, they worked out the details of what Howard hoped would be the first of many evenings they would spend together.

Chapter 28
Soviet Office to the United Nations, New York
October 10, 1950

Dmitry Abramenkov's assignment to the Soviet Consulate in New York was not meant to be. In July 1948, Oksana Kasenkina, a Soviet citizen and teacher to the children of diplomats assigned to the Soviet Mission to the United Nations, appealed to the editor of a Russian-language newspaper in New York City for refuge. As a result, arrangements were made to take Kasenkina to the Reed Farm in Valley Cottage, north of New York City. The Reed Farm was operated by the White Russian Tolstoy Foundation, formed by the daughter of Russian writer Leo Tolstoy to provide assistance to Russian refugees from the Soviet Union and Eastern Europe. In August, Soviet Consul-General Jacob Lomakin with Vice-Consul Chepurnykh arrived at the farm. According to the Tolstoy Foundation, Kasenkina freely returned to the consulate. Letters of protest by the Soviets alleging Kasenkina had been kidnapped and held against her will by members of the Tolstoy Foundation followed, resulting in both legal and political posturing by both sides. In August, the sordid affair took a different turn when Kasenkina jumped from the third-story window of the East 61st Street consulate and was hospitalized with serious injuries. In her own words, Kasenkina remarked she had a stronger desire for deliverance than for asylum. Ultimately, the incident and the deteriorating relationship between the two countries led to the closure of the Soviet consulate in New York, as well as their consulate in San Francisco in late August of 1948. In reciprocity, the Soviet Union ordered that the United States consulate in Vladivostok be closed, and plans for a U.S. consulate in Leningrad were shelved. The situation remained irreparable for nearly 26 years until 1974 when both countries came to an agreement to open consulates in their respective countries.

During World War II, which the Soviet's later referred to as their Great Patriotic War, the one-time allied nations proposed the establishment of an international body designed to maintain international peace and security and international economic and social cooperation after the war. The United Nations was officially established with the signing of its charter on October 24, 1945. Later that same year, the U.S. requested the U.N. be headquartered in the U.S., and the U.N. body accepted this suggestion. After considering several sites in and around New York City, it was decided the headquarters would be constructed along the East River. The U.N. headquarters officially opened in January 1951, although construction was not formally completed until October 1952. In 1948, Yakov Alexandrovich Malik, along with a small staff, was posted to New York as the Soviet's Permanent Representative. With the consulate closed for the foreseeable future, Dmitry was assigned to New York under the guise of working on Comrade Malik's mission staff.

After personal indoctrination from Colonel Sergei Shtemenko following his VDA training, Dmitry was posted to the Russian sector of Berlin for nearly two years to hone his tradecraft. Ever the best student, Dmitry excelled at handling sensitive contacts, and at agent development. Shtemenko was impressed by Dmitry's progress, confirming his selection of Dmitry to handle a highly sensitive and trusted agent in New York.

NORMAN, as Dmitry was known in coded cable traffic between New York and Moscow, was responsible for activating and handling agent BRAVE. Moscow had remained patient at Shtemenko's recommendation, and had not serviced BRAVE in the United States since his arrival in 1945. Shtemenko wanted BRAVE to become comfortable in his new life, and establish trust with U.S. officials minding everything in his daily life. Shtemenko couldn't have known he was one-hundred percent right, but his theory that BRAVE and others like him would be segregated from other scientists, and would have their phones monitored and mail censored was accurate. Shtemenko knew that eventually U.S. intelligence officials would become convinced BRAVE had become a loyal U.S. citizen, and would cut him loose from their oppressive chains. Shtemenko's theories were proven true when Moscow received a post card from BRAVE, posted from Jersey City, and mailed to an accommodation address in London belonging to another GRU agent. BRAVE had sent the post card in August 1950. It was now time for Dmitry to actively operate BRAVE and gain access to U.S. scientific secrets developed at Picatinny.

Chapter 29
NYU Campus
Evening of October 10, 1950

Howard entered NYU's Main Building into a sea of mostly men and a smattering of women. Howard had sat in the back during the lecture, understanding that Fran was busy assisting the professors who filled the panel discussion on Nuclear Theory. Howard, like most, was awed by the destructive power unleashed on Hiroshima and Nagasaki. Howard's technical radio operator training, which included radio communication and navigation, had given him an above average understanding of scientific principals, but like most, Howard only had a rudimentary understanding of the physics and mechanics behind unleashing ungodly devastation. To Howard, the panel's detached discussion of complicated scientific principals left him wondering if these men really understood what hold they held over precious life. Howard had read about Albert Einstein's own struggles with reconciling his involvement in developing the atomic bomb, but Howard was certain of one thing. He, and other men and women who had served their country during the war, knew that the use of such destruction had brought an end to a protracted war that had already taken the lives of over 300,000 soldiers, marines, and sailors. It had ultimately cost the lives of untold millions throughout Europe and Asia.

As Howard worked his way through the crowd, he bumped into a neatly dressed man with graying temples.

"Excuse me," the man uttered in an arrogant tone as he hurried past towards the hall's exit door. Howard noted a slight, but noticeably refined German accent in the man's voice. As Howard was about to offer an obligatory reply, he heard Fran calling his name from off to the right, causing him to quickly forget the encounter. Howard couldn't help but notice how beautiful Fran was in her red dress which set off her brilliant green eyes. Although Howard appreciated that Fran was the complete package, it was her eyes that always mesmerized him. "Hello Fran, you look stunning," Howard exclaimed as he finally reached his prize.

"Well, thank you kind sir," Fran replied with a bright smile and embrace. Howard didn't want to let her go, as he lingered and took in the intoxicating smell at the nape of her neck. As Howard pulled back from the embrace, he couldn't help notice an elderly man nearby dressed in a conservative suit jacket with vest and violet colored necktie. "My dear Fran, aren't you going to introduce me to this handsome and dashing young man?" The man said with a mischievous smile forming on his lips, framed by a perfectly groomed white mustache.

"Why yes," Fran replied. "This is Mr. Howard Brooks, who…" Fran paused realizing she didn't even know what Howard did for a living.

Howard immediately offered his hand, and filled in for Fran. "Good evening, please call me Howard, Sir. I'm a Special Agent with the FBI." As Howard's words left his lips, he noticed that Fran had a puzzled look on her face.

"Well, good evening to you also, Howard. My name is Doctor Julius Newberry. I'm the director of our college faculty.

I say, it's not every day you meet a G-man," Dr. Newberry exclaimed, again with a wry smile.

"No, it's not, is it," Fran retorted as she recovered from her initial shock. "I'm sorry Dr. Newberry, Howard and I met at the end of the war when he was on leave and heading home. We ran into each other this morning for the first time in many years. We still haven't had the time to catch up. I assumed he was working in the corporate world."

"That's right," Howard continued. "There is much we need to catch up on. I studied engineering at Iowa State and obtained my degree in short order. But life sometimes takes you in a different direction. Call it fate, destiny, or God's plan if you will. I joined the FBI in 1949 and got here to New York just this year. Running into Fran, literally," Howard said with a wry smile, "was unexpected, but an absolute pleasure," Howard continued as a genuine smile passed across his face as he looked into Fran's eyes.

"Well, young man, perhaps that was destiny also," Dr. Newberry jested as he touched Fran's arm. "Speaking of fate Howard, it looks like you could use a drink. How about going with Fran to the bar and retrieving me a neat Scotch while you're at it?"

"Most certainly, Sir," Howard replied with a slight bow as he took Fran's arm. However, they never did return to Dr. Newberry with the neat Scotch. Howard and Fran steered away from the crowd to catch up on time lost and became lost in each others' eyes.

Chapter 30
New York City
December, 1950

    Dmitry had worked hard over the past few months learning the New York City subterranean subway system, and numerous bus routes. The key to an intelligence officer's tradecraft working in a large and busy metropolis, was the ability to plan complicated and varied routes designed to detect surveillance by the host country's law enforcement or security services. Great lengths were taken to securely meet an agent or conduct one of a number of tradecraft operations designed to support such agents. Working in Germany was child's play compared to New York City, as the Soviet Union controlled a vast network of agents and cooperators in West Berlin. Dmitry knew the FBI and its source network created a hostile environment for an intelligence officer to operate. The FBI had cut its teeth on stakeouts of criminal gangs and organized crime, on the likes of Dillinger, Pretty Boy Floyd, and Al Capone. However, the FBI had really honed its surveillance craft during WWII by watching Nazi agents and saboteurs. Following the war, it was any easy switch for the FBI to target its new enemy.

    As a result, Dmitry had to design his operations to allow him to remain one step ahead of the FBI. He became adept at using cover stops such as shopping excursions on his way to Grand Central station or one of many smaller subway platforms. He would stop at large storefront windows, which acted as mirrors, to browse items on display. He would also go inside and peer out the same windows, from behind a display rack, to see who stopped outside to look in or see who followed him in as a fellow shopper. Dmitry knew if he stayed inside long enough, his pursuers couldn't fight human curiosity. Eventually, they would come inside to confirm whether or not he had really entered. Identifying stores with more than one point of egress was preferred, but couldn't be used too often as the FBI would soon become witting of his ploy. Dmitry also planned his routes to include several subway or train station platform changes, and often used the bus to lose his tail. Most importantly, Dmitry began to set a weekday and weekend pattern designed to lull the FBI into complacency. The key was to force the FBI into assuming he was only following a daily routine of menial and dull tasks. In reality, Dmitry's pattern was designed to create small opportunities where he could either perform an operational task under the noses of the FBI or create enough of a buffer that he could exploit and disappear into thin air.

    Dmitry preferred meeting his agents and conducting supporting operations on weekends. Dmitry knew the FBI staffed fewer agents on weekends, as many had families. Dmitry set a pattern early upon his arrival in New York City. He and Tatiana would set out at a reasonable time in the morning from their 3rd floor walk-up apartment located near the Soviet Mission on Park Avenue and 68th Street. They would walk for a few blocks to the same small café on 6th Avenue, just south of Central Park. There, they would share coffee and exchange sections of The New York Times. Reading The Times allowed Dmitry to further advance his English skills while simultaneously allowing him to check for surveillance. It was common for followers to tire of stops for long breakfasts and lunches. Often, Dmitry found his assigned team would break the perimeter and join him and Tatiana at the local café, or park their car on the street close by to take the "eye". Whether he had a team assigned to him that day did not matter. Dmitry was trained to work in the gap, the window of time and distance allowing an intelligence officer to conduct tradecraft or lose a tail before detection. After coffee, they would walk the same route towards a group of food stalls at the lower end of Central Park, pausing many times to identify surveillance operatives. Their routine journey these many Saturday mornings would continue south through Manhattan, always along the same streets with the same cover stops. Dmitry was convinced his route would maximize his ability to detect surveillance, or better yet, lull the FBI into believing he was only out for a Saturday with the lovely Tatiana. Dmitry was in control, because he would pick and choose which Saturday he would go operational.

Chapter 31
FBI New York Office
June 1951

"Gentlemen, have a seat," Supervisory Special Agent Marcus Robinson said to Howard, Jack, and several other counterespionage agents as they filed into the conference room. Although not nearly a command, Robinson's voice was filled with gravity. "As you know, with the formal move of the United Nations to its new home in New York, the Soviet intelligence services have seized an opportunity to expand its presence under the cover as diplomats posted from their government's Ministry of Foreign Affairs. The threat posed by the KGB and GRU has increased exponentially, and we must be prepared to counter this threat with sophisticated operations and tactics. Let me introduce you to SSA William Lamphere from Headquarters. Some of you know Bill from his first office assignment here in New York. Understand that Bill's message comes directly from Director Hoover. Pay attention, Gentlemen. Our country's national security is at stake."

"Good morning, Gentlemen. I wish I could say it is good to be back in New York, but the information I'm going to impart on you leaves no room for such sentiments. What I'm about to provide you comes with the highest of classifications and all will be required to sign a Non-Disclosure Agreement (NDA) before we continue," Lamphere advised as SSA Robinson began to hand out the forms to the five men seated at the table. "Let me stress the importance of what we are about to discuss in this room comes with the personal attention of the Director, and any violations of the NDA without express permission will be deemed a terminable offense. Am I clear on that point, gentlemen?" Lamphere asked, waiting in turn as Howard, Jack, and the others acknowledged his watchful eye with a nod as Lamphere personally collected each NDA. "I'm not at liberty to discuss the original source of this information, but I assure you, it has passed all measures of scrutiny. In late 1949, we learned of a GRU officer codenamed NORMAN who was to be assigned to the United States. Our best analysts have pored over past and current investigations conducted by you, and agents assigned to monitor activities at the Soviet Embassy in Washington. To date, we have not further identified NORMAN. In addition, we are in receipt of information indicating several GRU agents have been either sent to the United States, or even more alarming, have been developed here. These agents are known as KORN, MORSE, and BRAVE. Complicating this situation is what SSA Robinson led with upon calling this meeting to order. Not knowing precisely when or where NORMAN was posted, the potential of additional cover KGB and GRU officers assigned to the Soviet Mission to the United Nations, or SMUN as we are now referring to it, has only muddied the intelligence. Gentlemen, each of you has been personally selected to work on a special team formed with the express purposes of identifying NORMAN and his GRU agents, indentifying the threat posed by their operations, and neutralizing this threat. I cannot adequately express the gravity of the situation, Gentlemen. We cannot fail. You are now assigned to SSA Robinson to work exclusively on this matter which we have codenamed RED EYE. Now, let's get into the details.

Chapter 32
New York City
December 15, 1951

Days turned to weeks, and weeks to months. An Indian Summer had extended the mild weather late into the fall. Nonetheless, winter had finally taken hold. Howard and Jack had been at it now for weeks; sitting in a car, or if you were lucky, a café, as conducting surveillance was tedious and downright boring. You had to fight the human tendency of becoming complacent. Where you position yourself, how well you blend into your environment, and vigilant observation are key. The target clearly had the advantage, and an Agent needed to remain sharp and focused if he was to effectively follow the target without detection. Howard's commitment to advancing the goals of RED EYE had not wavered, but the initial excitement had clearly worn off. Day after day, shift after shift, and hour after hour without tangible results had worn the team down.

On this particular Saturday, the team had been assigned to follow Dmitry Abramenkov, which had to be their fourth or fifth such time, Howard thought. Abramenkov's routine on Saturday's had already been identified by the team. Howard was positioned at a small street café located on 6th Avenue, a few yards south of Abramenkov and his wife. The couple sat at a small bistro table conversing over coffee and The New York Times. The team knew the Abramenkovs particularly liked this café on Saturdays. They looked genuinely happy to Howard, making it even harder for him to focus as his mind drifted off towards his own relationship with

Fran. Their schedules had become increasingly difficult to align, especially with Howard's sporadic shifts.

Howard and Fran's relationship had taken off like a rocket, a topic in which Fran was well versed and often brought into their discussions. Fran's PhD work had progressed nicely over the course of the year and Howard was impressed by her passion for all things in the physical world. Howard had never known a woman like Fran, who could be an independent thinker and academic on one hand, and the perfect date on the other. Howard had quickly fallen in love, and he was sure Fran felt the same way. Conveniently for the two of them, Jack was increasingly absent from their shared apartment, often working overtime or seeing a number of women. Still the playboy, at least Jack had taken to not sharing all the lurid details of his dating life; something Howard had found himself becoming much less interested in, now having found his true love. With Jack gone most nights, Howard and Fran were able to relax alone and without interruption. Fran's own living arrangement of sharing an apartment near campus with two undergraduates was not conducive to privacy, nor was Howard's working Saturdays on most weekends in support of RED EYE. However, if all went well, Howard would be able to keep a late dinner date with Fran.

As Howard regained his focus on the task at hand, he noticed the Abramenkovs had walked away from their table and were entering a corner pharmacy, a few store fronts further north at 58th Street. Howard set off at a panicked pace, throwing a dollar bill on the table and not waiting for change. Howard knew their team had been spread thin that morning, having to cover two targets on this Saturday. But

Howard took solace in knowing Jack was in their car parked on the cross street about 40 yards due west of the pharmacy. So, he paused outside the entrance door and used his skills as a runner to catch his breath and slow his pulse. Howard had to fight the desire to enter the pharmacy, knowing Abramenkov would use the opportunity to identify his tail. In addition, he knew he had to reposition himself from a viewpoint which would conceal his position. But after a few minutes, Howard grew increasingly uncomfortable, knowing that if Abramenkov had exited the pharmacy undetected, the odds of reacquiring their prey would diminish greatly.

    Howard approached the entrance door, pausing to open it for a young mother pulling a reluctant small boy. She and the boy would provide Howard some cover as he would give Abramenkov and his wife the impression they were a family. However, when Howard cleared the threshold, he immediately realized a second egress point was located on the cross street. Howard scanned the pharmacy, and not seeing the Abramenkovs, he made for the door located on the north side. Howard slowly exited and leaned out slightly to afford himself some cover within the recessed entrance. Howard quickly glanced right and then left, but Abramenkov was nowhere in sight. Howard was stunned and confused. After the Abramenkovs had entered the store, Howard had positioned himself to the east, and he was convinced they had not come his way or headed north up 6th Avenue. Howard concluded they must have headed west towards Jack's position. But as Howard approached their Bureau car, Jack was still positioned behind the wheel with a look of startled confusion on his own face.

Jack exited as Howard approached. "Why are you here, where is Abramenkov?" Jack quickly asked with alarm in his voice. Howard stared incredulously back at Jack. "You mean you didn't see them heading your way from the corner pharmacy?" Howard asked with confusion.

"No, there is no way they came this way. I was looking east this whole time," Jack countered with heat building in his voice.

"Oh, shit. They've disappeared and they have at least a five minute head start," Howard replied deflated, knowing he had blown the surveillance and would have to answer directly to Robinson.

Chapter 33
New York Office of the FBI
Same Day

Howard stole a glance at his Waltham aviator's watch as SSA Robinson paced the floor of the conference room. The watch was a fond reminder of Crew 64, his first team. Howard couldn't imagine dropping the ball while aboard the Liberty Belle. Life and death depended on each doing their assigned task to the fullest.

The team had reassembled late afternoon following the debacle losing Abramenkov. Howard knew he and Jack were most responsible, and he fully accepted blame. Howard had been raised in a household built on trust, honor, and responsibility. Mistakes would be made, and hell would always need to be paid. What bothered Howard most was Jack's insistence Abramenkov had not come his way. Howard had done the math over and over in his mind. Math was exact, and as a derivative, so was engineering, Howard's academic discipline. Howard simply couldn't find any other solution to the problem of Abramenkov's vanishing act. He must have exited the door on 58th Street and headed west towards Jack. The pharmacy had no basement or other exit doors, and both he and Jack had searched the stockroom to no avail.

"How the hell did you two knuckleheads lose Abramenkov and his wife right under your noses?" Robinson barked rhetorically, clearly not looking for an answer. "I'll tell you how. You were clearly daydreaming or sleeping behind the wheel. You two blockheads let your team down, you let me down, you let Director Hoover down, and worst yet, you let America down. Now get out of my sight. I want a detailed report of today's activities down to how much sugar he used in his coffee, how many stirs with the spoon and taps on the cup rim, and whether or not he prefers to hold his wife's left or right hand. I even want to know which side he prefers to slide his Johnson when he crosses his legs. And I want it in triplicate and on my desk for review before any of you leave this storied office. Do I make myself clear Gentlemen? Do I?!" Robinson bellowed, not expecting an answer as he turned to exit, slamming the conference room door behind him.

"This one's on me, Fellas," Howard advised, looking each man of the team in the eye, including Jack. I'm sorry I ruined your Saturday night," Howard exclaimed with clear sincerity in his voice. All then rose from the table in unison, not stating the obvious or belaboring the point. However, each knew that it could have happened to any one of them. Howard and Jack were the last to exit, walking in silence towards their desks.

Howard sat at the typewriter and inserted the paper with carbons positioned in-between as Jack walked past, only to return with two steaming cups of coffee in stained China mugs. "Howard, you shouldn't have taken the brunt of the blame back there. I obviously missed Abramenkov coming my way. I keep going over it again and again, and the only result I get is that the two of them must have crossed 58th Street in front of traffic and used the park cars for cover as they slipped past me," Jack offered with a conciliatory tone.

"Jack, we're partners and we take the blame together. No doubt we screwed up. But we won't let that happen again, no way, now how," Howard stated as he rub his temples with his thumbs. "Man, Fran's going to be upset. This will be the second Saturday in a row I've stood her up. I'd better call her so she can make other plans, maybe with one of those strapping young grad students she tutors on the side," Howard said with his eyes closed. He knew Fran would never really do such a thing, even to send him a message that they had not yet committed to each other for the long term. Howard had been toying with the idea of proposing to Fran. He clearly loved her, and when he tallied the pros and cons of spending the rest of his life with Fran, marriage always came out the overwhelming winner. However, Howard knew his career with the FBI was demanding and he was aware of the possibility that he could always be transferred to headquarters or some backwater posting without much notice. He also knew Fran's work was equally as important as his, and he didn't want to force her into choosing between the two.

"Howard," Jack began, bringing Howard back to the present, "we better get cracking or we won't get out of here before midnight, Old Man," Jack offered, knowing Howard was thinking of Fran and losing focus. "Place that call and I'll warm up our coffees."

Chapter 34
Abramenkov's Apartment, NYC
Later that Night

Abramenkov and his wife had arrived home early evening after his successful operational run. After using the pharmacy as a cover stop, they had exited through the north door out onto 58th Street, using the recessed doorway as a temporary hide. They waited for a large box truck lumbering down the street towards their position before running across 58th in front of it and towards a doorway on the opposite side of the street. The Abramenkovs paused only temporarily in the new doorway, knowing they only had moments before their tailing FBI friends would grow suspicious and start after them. Peering out from the doorway looking west, Abramenkov noted a lone occupied dark sedan parked farther up the street, with the driver facing their direction. Abramenkov paused only for a few more moments, waiting for additional vehicular and pedestrian traffic to obscure the sedan driver's vision before he and Tatiana hastily headed west. Abramenkov used his peripheral vision only to sneak a peek in the sedan's direction as they scurried past. He noted the driver appeared to be oblivious to their escape.

Needing to confirm they had truly shaken their tail, the Abramenkovs continued west and south in a stair step pattern used to weed out surveillance on foot. Abramenkov also used two additional cover stops before entering the 59th Street subway station and taking the N Train due south towards Union Square. At the 34th Street/Herald Square station, they exited, crossed the platform and headed back north; only again to exit, cross the platform, and again head south. They arrived at the 14th Street/Union Square Station and entered the Strand Bookstore on 4th Avenue. Once inside, Dmitry split from Tatiana, leaving her in the Russian languages section, an area not typically frequented during these times of the Red Scare. Tatiana would later report that she detected no one checking on her activities, or otherwise resembling a surveillance operative. Dmitry had trained Tatiana himself, and her keen attention to detail made her the perfect decoy.

After leaving Tatiana, Dmitry stopped at a Hudson news stand to purchase the day's copy of The Saturday Evening Post. Besides filling his requirement for a parole, Dmitry often enjoyed a later reading the Post. He admired the cover work by Norman Rockwell, a truly gifted man with an innate ability to capture the human essence. Assured by his tradecraft he was operating in the clear, Dmitry continued his journey, culminating with a visit at one of NYU's many disjointed campus libraries. Dmitry browsed a few topical sections before entering the Applied Sciences stack. He then appeared to haphazardly drop his copy of the Post on the floor, while retrieving a 1939 copy of The Biology of the Cell Surface by American biologist Ernest E. Just from the stack. As he bent to retrieve the Post, BRAVE bent as well to offer assistance.

"Here, let me help you," Wilhelm Bauer offered. "I say, is that last week's Post with the article WOMEN ARE NEVER SATISFIED by Stee McNeil?" Bauer asked.

"No, I'm sorry to say. This is the current copy," Abramenkov replied.

Having exchanged the proper paroles indicating both were in the clear and uncompromised, Bauer dropped an envelope on top of Abramenkov's Post; and as they both started to rise, Abramenkov slipped the envelope and its contents inside the newspaper. Having accomplished the exchange, they departed in opposite directions with only moments passing since their encounter.

Back home, and with the adrenaline from today's activities finally clearing his system, Dmitry slumped into his favorite chair as Tatiana dutifully offered him a glass of Smirnoff vodka retrieved from the icebox. The adrenaline dump had finally waned and he felt exhausted by the ordeal.

"Were we successful today Dima, my handsome love?" Tatiana asked as she bent to kiss Dmitry on the cheek.

"Yes, my love. We were once again," Dmitry replied as he pulled Tatiana into his lap with a smile broadening across his face and finding new energy.

Chapter 35
Howard and Jack's Apartment, NYC
December 20, 1951

Fran lay across the couch with her head in Howard's lap. They had finished an early dinner and had the apartment to themselves, as Jack was normally absent these days. "You out did yourself tonight, Fran," Howard exclaimed as he sipped on a Scotch over ice. "But you have to stop making such wonderful desserts. I'm not sure I can run enough miles to keep up with your apparent attempt to fatten me up. Somehow, I feel you are leading me to the slaughter."

"Well, now that you mention it. Mother and Father insist you come out to Brooklyn on Christmas Eve for dinner and festivities. After you cancelled on us on Thanksgiving, Mother is starting to worry and Father has begun questioning your intentions. And by the way, no one forced you to eat a second piece of my cheesecake," Fran countered with playfulness in her voice.

"Oh, come on now Fran, you know Robinson had us working over the Thanksgiving holiday," Howard offered, and then paused before continuing. "Fran, we need to talk," Howard continued, causing her to pull herself upright and create some distance between the two of them. Fran's face displayed worry in anticipation of some bad news. "Fran, we've been seeing each other for some time now, and I understand how your folks and you are starting to wonder about where all of this is heading. I've never met a more wonderful and beautiful woman in my life, but..." Howard started but was cut off by Fran.

"But what Howard? Is this 'the talk'? You've done a great job of using work as an excuse lately to cancel many dates. Just be honest with me, Howard. Exactly where are we exactly going with all of this?" Fran stated more than asked. "A relationship can't be built on just one willing party," Fran continued.

"Fran, please let me finish. I want nothing more than to spend my time with you and only you. But work has been very crazy as of late, and I don't ever see an end in sight. And the worst part, I can't tell you what I'm doing. It pains me to cancel our dates, and I know my calls must just seem like excuses. But please trust me Fran, the work I'm doing is very important and I believe I'm involved for a reason. It's nothing I can explain; it's more of a gut feeling, really. Call if fate, destiny, God's plan, if you will. But Fran, I don't see my schedule changing anytime soon. The work I do in national security for the FBI is very demanding and the hours will never fit that of a regular day job. Working long hours, nights, weekends and holidays will always be the 'norm' for me. I know it's not fair of me to ask you to understand and to get used to disappointment. And I won't. And your career Fran, your PhD work and teaching at NYU also creates crazy hours. I would never impede your pursuit of your own plans. If this isn't the kind of life you want to live, if you want a more traditional relationship, I understand. But let me know now so each of us can avoid a lot of heartache," Howard said with both a sense of relief having finally broached the topic, and trepidation if Fran took his offer and bailed.

Fortunately, Howard's anxiety quickly dissolved as Fran pulled in close with a sly smile on her beautiful lips. "Oh Howard, I was worried you didn't want me. I don't care about the silly hours and demands, as long as we have time for each other when we're not at work. Howard, I'm committed to you. Go ahead and call this fate or destiny, we can make this work. I love you, Darling."

"Oh Babe, I love you too!" Howard whispered in Fran's ear as he began to unzip her dress. Thank you Jack for not being around again.

Chapter 36
Picatinny Arsenal, New Jersey
December 23, 1951

Bauer bode his time well, waiting for the party to hit its full stride before he slipped out from the cafeteria, and shuffled down the hallway towards the lab. The Christmas spirit, and alcohol, was a great distraction from what he was about to do. In addition, the holiday break would mean a long weekend with minimal staff, the perfect scenario for slipping back into the laboratory building at the arsenal to return the plans.

Bauer's Soviet handlers had been pressing him to copy the schematics for the ultra-secret Nike rocket anti-aircraft missile system originally developed by Bell Laboratories in Murray Hill, NJ. Bauer had devoted much of his time to the project over the past few months, as the rocket's early designs were based on German engineering.

Bauer had refused to use the Minox camera issued to him by NORMAN for this job. The size of the plans meant he would have to take several overlapping photos of each page at equal distance in order for the GRU to reassemble the drawings, which would take too much time and create too much exposure. His handlers may not be happy with the result, and ask him to repeat the process. No, Bauer thought it much less risky to wait for the holiday break to remove and return the plans when no one would be working for a few days. NORMAN had assured him the GRU could copy and return the plans to Bauer by the next day. By Bauer's calculations, he would only need three days to pull off the operation. He had established a pattern of working early or late, and popping in on Sundays from time to time to catch up on work. Most viewed Bauer's additional hours as obsessive or the mark of a German eccentric, but not as suspicious. Bauer understood the American approach to work which still bothered his German sensibilities. American's would seize any excuse to take time off from their work, and since Bauer had lost his faith in God and man after separation from his wife and daughter, he was not interested in celebrating the birth of Christ.

A broken heart and stress from spying for the Soviets aside, Bauer had begun, on some level, to appreciate his life in America. He was well respected at work, and his salary allowed him to provide a good life and promising future for his son. Bauer had taken an Adjunct Professor position at NYU, teaching a physics course for undergraduate students on Saturdays. The position came with two main perks. First, when Johan graduated high school in the spring, he would enroll at NYU at a great discount. Second, the weekend visits to the NYU campus conveniently gave him reason to be in the city for meets with NORMAN.

Regardless, Bauer never forgot he wasn't in complete control of such matters or of his life in general. His Soviet handlers knew he would continue to perform even if reuniting with his lovely Giselle and young Elsa was so remote a possibility. He knew he must continue for the slimmest measure of hope; and although they had never directly threatened Johan, Bauer knew the Soviet machine and their Communist wickedness knew no boundaries.

Chapter 37
NYU Campus
Christmas Eve, 1951 (Mid-morning)

Removing the plans from the arsenal had gone well with only one slight incident. The cheating hearts and hands of Dr. Johnson and his secretary, heading for the good doctor's secluded and dark office, caused Bauer a moment of alarm. Preoccupied with blind lust, they paid him little mind as they passed by Bauer, groping each other like teenagers. Bauer wondered how either would reconcile their thoughts as they celebrated Christmas morning with their spouses and young children. Such people and their wickedness bothered Bauer. Wasn't marriage a sacred institution?

Bauer rolled the plans and placed them in a rigid cardboard tube wrapped in bright Christmas paper and an ornate red bow for appearances. Bauer had brought the tube to the office several weeks earlier, casually explaining to all who asked that he had bought an early Christmas gift of a collapsible fishing rod set for Johan and wanted to keep it from the prying eyes of a teenager. With the trust Bauer had established with his fellow researches and staff, no one questioned the love of a widowed father for his only son.

Entering the shared Adjunct office on campus, Bauer was surprised to see Miss Fran Dwyer walking towards him in the corridor. "Merry Christmas, Dr. Bauer! I'm surprised to see you today with much of the campus deserted because of the holidays," Fran expressed without suspicion in her voice. Nevertheless, Bauer was prepared for such an encounter.

"Same to you, Miss Dwyer. I thought I would stop in for a couple of hours to get a jump on preparing my next lecture. Besides, my son Johan is spending the day with a school mate's family skiing in the Poconos and won't be back until early evening. We have plans to meet at Rockefeller Center early evening to see the beautiful Christmas tree so many have suggested I not miss," Bauer said delivering his cover story. "And you, Miss Dwyer. What brings you into these hallowed halls before the holidays? Shouldn't you be at home, relaxing and enjoying your family on such a glorious day?" Bauer asked.

"Well, I'm as guilty as you Dr. Bauer. I thought I would get in a few hours grading the semester exams which were given before the holidays. My mind is always turning and turning, and I want to celebrate the holidays without worry. Besides, I won't be heading to Brooklyn until this evening," Fran explained.

"Well, I guess great minds find no rest, Miss Dwyer. Merry Christmas and happy holidays," Bauer exclaimed with a smile as he entered the office, not waiting for further small talk nor wanting to engage anyone further as he held the secret plans in his hands.

As Fran continued down the corridor, she paid no further attention to the brief encounter, instead returning her focus to the task at hand so she could clear her mind and enjoy her first real holiday with Howard.

Chapter 38
New York City
Christmas Eve, 1951 (Late Afternoon)

"Well, look who decided to pop in for once," Howard jested as Jack entered through the door, carrying shopping bags from Macy's and FOA Schwartz. Jack's presence at the apartment had been scarce the last couple of months between work and extracurricular activities. Howard often wondered where Jack got all the energy. Howard thought the bag from the famous toy store curious.

"Merry Christmas to you too, Old Man," Jack replied with a smile on his face as they embraced and exchanged Christmas greetings.

"I can't thank you enough, Jack, for lobbying with Marcus to get me the night off to spend with Fran. This means the world to me. Sorry you have to work though. You'd think the office would make an exception for the holiday and give everyone a break."

"Don't sweat it, Howard. I actually convinced Robinson to give all the 'married' guys the night off," Jack said while emphasizing married. "There are enough of us bachelors out there to take care of business. Besides, you and Fran practically are married by the way the two of you have been carrying on. Really Howard, when are you going to make an honest woman out of her and stop sullying the Dwyers' good name?" Jack continued as he removed his fedora, overcoat, and galoshes.

"Well, now that you mention it. Take a look at this," Howard replied as he pulled a small blue box from his suit jacket. As Howard opened the box, the apartment's dim light was enough to cause the solitaire center stone to sparkle with brilliance. Howard waited expectedly for Jack to comment.

"It's beautiful, Howard. Are you going to do it tonight, Old Man? In front of her parents, no doubt?" Jack said, already assuming the answer. "This will be a Christmas to remember and no way to top it."

"You bet, Jack. I knew from the minute I met Fran back at that USO club in '45 that she was the one. I remember talking to Captain Hassig and other married guys from our squadron about how they each knew their wife was the one out of all the girls they had dated. The shared response from Hassig and others, those who you could tell were truly committed, you know, the ones who didn't see being over there as a license to chase any skirt that moved... Each answered with a simple, 'you'll just know.' Well Jack, that's the way it was with Fran. I guess I just had to find her again, that's all."

"Congratulations, Howard! I'm so happy for the two of you. Oh man, would you look at the time. I need to get up on set by 1800 or Robinson will have it in for me," Jack exclaimed as he brushed past Howard to conduct a quick shirt change and swallow down a few gulps of day old cold coffee from the percolator.

Howard took one last look at the ring before snapping the lid shut and returning the box to his pocket, patting it a few times to make sure it was safe and secure. "A Christmas to remember, indeed," Howard thought as he grabbed his overcoat, donned his hat, and headed for the door.

Chapter 39
New York City, Area of Rockefeller Center Christmas Eve, 1951 (Early Evening)

Dmitry Abramenkov and his wife had left their apartment early afternoon under the auspices of last minute Christmas shoppers. The usual stop for coffee at the same familiar café was already checked off their list as they made their way south on 5th Avenue towards a small art shop selling posters of iconic city landmarks to tourists. This was no fancy art gallery by any stretch of the imagination, but no one would expect a mid-level Soviet Vice-Consul to shop at anything nicer. The contents of the shop were irrelevant, according to Dmitry's plan. His goal was to buy any of the popular posters sold at a never ending "discount" and rolled into a cardboard tube for protection from the winter elements. Of course, Dmitry accepted the store manager's offer to wrap the gift for free in festive paper with a large red bow.

With this part of his operational plan achieved, Dmitry and Tatiana continued south towards Macy's on 34th Street. They stopped to take in ornately decorated store windows with throngs of other shoppers and tourists, out for a taste of Christmas spirit. The overcast but dry day allowed Dmitry to use the display windows as mirrors to confirm his tail was still with them. For today's operation, losing the tail was not necessary, unless their pursuer's own bumbling allowed them to carry on free of detection. No, today Dmitry could achieve his goal by using the crowds to work in the gap, that small window of time and space that would allow him to conduct the brush pass with his agent BRAVE.

Dmitry "reluctantly" entered Macy's as Tatiana playfully tugged on his arm. He then dutifully followed her around from one department to the next, finally settling on a new pullover sweater in dull grey. God forbid, if there was a God, Dmitry thought, that Tatiana would be allowed to buy something bright and festive as such gaiety was frowned upon by Communist and Soviet ideals. For once, he would like for her to be allowed to wear one of those low cut button down sweaters popularized by the current screen sirens. After all, Tatiana's figure was still very desirable to Dmitry, and to any red blooded man, for that matter. Focus, Dmitry thought to himself, as the enormity of today's operation returned to the forefront of his mind.

Dmitry stole a quick glance at his wrist watch and noted the anointed hour quickly approaching. They must start out soon for Rockefeller Center to allow ample time for slow sidewalk traffic and congested intersections. Tatiana finished her purchase with a sigh; for she also knew the sweater would be just one more added to a drawer of other dull and muted choices. Dmitry asked for a large bag to accommodate their purchase and the wrapped tube he was carrying. The store clerk was happy to help, flashing a big smile so typical of an American. Why do they smile so much? Dmitry wondered. He was convinced most of it was insincere.

Before exiting the store, Dmitry and Tatiana stopped by the ladies and men's restrooms to avail themselves of the free admission, having completed a purchase. Dmitry quickly entered a stall, removed the print from the tube, folded it, and concealed it inside a large pocket Tatiana had sewn inside his overcoat. Then he removed a collapsible fishing rod and small tackle from within the lining of his overcoat and placed them inside the tube.

As they exited Macy's and began to walk both north and east, Dmitry was quick to pick up the FBI surveillance team. Dmitry had counted only four since they set out on their journey from their apartment. Dmitry had purposely chosen Christmas Eve, knowing the team would be at minimum staff and preoccupied with thoughts of parties with friends and Christmas morning rituals with family. As they approached the Christmas tree positioned above the ice skating rink, Dmitry and Tatiana took up a position at the railing to ostensibly watch the twirling skaters putting on a show for the very large crowd of tourists. The dull daylight had quickly given way to a dark night clouded by a building bank of fog. The forecast called for icy rain mixed with snow and some accumulation overnight. A white Christmas for the Americans and their silly constant smiles, Dmitry thought. Little did anyone know, especially Abramenkov's minders, that Dmitry's most prized gift would soon be in his hands; for BRAVE was scheduled to be in the same area that night.

From their vantage point, Dmitry, with Tatiana's help, located the position of all four members of their surveillance team. Unfortunately for the team, their positions would not allow much maneuverability and time to react to Dmitry and Tatiana's quick move. Without fail, Dmitry spied BRAVE walking towards the tree with a tall handsome young man. Curious Dmitry thought, BRAVE was getting bolder in his actions by including his son in their little operation. Perhaps a good sign for future tasking for even more sensitive materials, Dmitry thought. It was his turn to lead Tatiana by the arm and start the most crucial and timed move of tonight's tasking.

Chapter 40
Rockefeller Center
Christmas Eve, 1951 (H-Hour)

Jack was in charge of tonight's team and was not shy about the fact. "Okay, listen up guys. No one moves unless you get the sign from me. If our boy moves off that railing, I will take the eye. No matter what, keep your eyes on that Macy's bag he's carrying. We don't want any surprises," Jack quickly and tersely issued the orders. Each man then spread out to cover all the logical egresses while Jack remained best positioned to see any movement.

The team was in place and had the area covered, as well as a small team of four agents could. Just short of 1800 hours, Jack saw Dmitry move off the railing, join the crowd, and walk closer to the tree. He and Tatiana then started to circle the tree counter-clockwise against the wave of the masses caught in what looked like a human whirlpool to Jack. He moved with them, motioning for his team to stay put. Jack was not going to leave anything to chance this time out, sacrificing exposure to ensure they had Dmitry covered. Jack was still stinging from the embarrassment he felt after receiving playful ridicule at the hands of the other teams members after the foul up at the pharmacy.

The crowd posed a greater challenge than Jack anticipated and he lost sight of Dmitry for only a few moments before again acquiring his prey. Jack found Dmitry and Tatiana stopped and standing back off the tree, gazing upwards at the bright star affixed to the top. Crisis avoided! Jack thought.

Chapter 41
Inside the Soviet U.N. Office, NYC
Christmas Eve, 1951 (1900 hours)

Having successfully executed the brush pass with BRAVE, Dmitry and Tatiana entered the Consulate and a party in full swing. Once inside, Dmitry entered the special room limited in access to GRU and Ministry of State Security (MGB) personnel. Dmitry found the GRU Colonel Viktor Karpov, the chief GRU officer or Resident in New York, waiting impatiently inside, obviously nervous over the night's events. Dmitry had come to view Karpov as nothing more than a bureaucrat working way above his skill set. Dmitry's mentor, Colonel Sergei Shtemenko, had warned him about the Resident, having revealed that Karpov only received his posting due to favoritism.

"Ah, Comrade Abramenkov," Karpov exclaimed trying to conceal his obvious nervousness. "I see you have finally returned. Let's see the package," he stammered.

Dmitry detected alcohol on the Resident's breath, which only compounded his ineptness. Nevertheless, Dmitry had performed well and he would let nothing sully his good mood.

Chapter 42
Outside the Soviet Mission, NYC
Christmas Eve, 1951 (1930 hours)

"Okay guys, let's call this thing," Jack said. "Everyone who is anyone is inside having a wonderful Christmas celebration while we freeze outside," he continued. A separate team covering the SMUN that evening had advised Jack and the others that about every employee attached to the Consulate and other Soviet offices had been showing up all night and entering with food and drink. "I'll write the reports the day after tomorrow. Merry Christmas everyone, get home safely," Jack offered, as all shook each other's hands and exchanged Christmas greetings, finally able to relax and head home to enjoy the holiday.

What all on the team apparently failed to realize were two fundamental facts about the 'Christmas' party supposedly in full-swing inside. First, the few Soviets who actually celebrate Christmas are Eastern Orthodox Christians who will celebrate nearly two weeks later, based on the Gregorian Calendar. Second, those who actually practice their religion do so quietly, as such public displays of religious leanings are not only frowned upon by the Communist Party and Soviet State, but are often persecuted.

Chapter 43
The Dwyer Residence
Brooklyn, New York
Christmas Eve, 1951

"Dinner was wonderful, Mrs. Dwyer. Thank you for inviting me into your home on such a blessed evening," Howard exclaimed as he placed the silverware on top of the fine China plate. The table was adorned with garland, fine settings, and Christmas cheer.

"Howard, we realize you must miss your family most during the holidays. Please understand you are always welcome," Mrs. Dwyer replied as she began to clear the table with the help of Fran. Fran just smiled in Howard's direction and gave him a little wink.

Wow, she looks so beautiful tonight, Howard thought to himself, as a smile spread across his face giving away his inner thoughts. Mr. Dwyer stood and turned, most certainly on his way to his den for an after dinner brandy. "Mr. Dwyer, if I may..." Howard started, only to be interrupted by Mr. Dwyer.

"Howard, would you care to join me for a brandy in my study?"

"I would enjoy that very much, Sir," Howard replied as he followed Mr. Dwyer down the grand hallway. As they moved down the hallway, since the Dwyers had adorned nearly every bit of the hallway's wall space with family photos, Howard could almost see Fran grow right before his very eyes.

As they entered study, Howard was struck by the opulence and wealth of the family. The many silver plaques and cups detailed the Dwyers' very successful accounting firm, along with the family's connections to some very important New York politicians and celebrities. As Mr. Dwyer poured each a small glass from a crystal decanter, Howard paced a bit nervously as he took in the scene.

"Here you go, my boy," Mr. Dwyer said as he offered Howard the drink. "I say Howard, you look a bit pre-occupied. Something on your mind? Perhaps you're wondering if you made the right choice choosing Mr. Hoover's agency over a career that truly exploits your degree field?" Mr. Dwyer asked with a bit of good natured ribbing.

"No, not really, Mr. Dwyer. I'm quite comfortable with my decision. My career with the FBI feels natural, as if I was brought onto God's green earth to do this very thing. But I must admit, I can clearly see that your own pursuits in the field of accounting have brought your family good fortune." Howard paused for a moment as he collected his thoughts, a situation quite obvious to Mr. Dwyer.

"Howard, is there something else on your mind? I couldn't help but notice you were a bit pre-occupied at dinner and that you barely touched Mrs. Dwyer's best Christmas ham," Mr. Dwyer exclaimed as he took a sip of his brandy.

"Actually Sir, there is something weighing heavily on my mind. Mr. Dwyer, when I returned from the war, I didn't quite know what I was going to do with myself. I was certain of very few things. I was at ease knowing attending university and pursuing my interests was in my future, but not quite sure where such pursuits would take me. Coming here to New York was not planned, but felt right, Mr. Dwyer. I don't know if I'm making much sense, but I now understand that coming here to work for the FBI was part of God's plan, destiny, fate, or whatever you want to call it. What I'm most certain of in life is one thing... Meeting your daughter was the best thing that could ever happen to me. Her smiling face and warm heart welcomed me back from some ungodly things I witnessed and experienced during the war; and running into Fran on the NYU campus, I feel was certainly part of God's plan, Mr. Dwyer."

Howard cleared his throat and took a sip of the brandy, looking for some relief for his dry throat. "Sir, I cannot imagine a future without Fran. With your permission Sir, I plan on proposing to Fran tonight."

A smile spread across Mr. Dwyer's face as he raised his glass to Howard. "Welcome to the family Howard, and from now forward, you may call me Dad," Mr. Dwyer said as he clinked his glass to Howard's. The tension in the room immediately evaporated as the amber liquid quickly warmed Howard's throat.

Chapter 44
NYC to Hoboken, NJ
Christmas Day Morning, 1951

Howard and a few others from the team were assigned the Christmas morning surveillance shift on Abramenkov. Howard didn't mind, he had spent an incredible night with Fran, culminating with Fran sneaking into the Dwyers' guest room for an early morning tryst.

As Howard sat in the driver's seat of the black FBI sedan, sipping his third cup of hot coffee, he thought back to the previous evening's wonder. After emerging from Mr. Dwyer's den, Howard and "Dad" joined Mrs. Dwyer, Fran, and Fran's younger brother at the family's Christmas tree. Mrs. Dwyer had laid out an assortment of scrumptious Christmas cookies and candies, and all had a full glass of a fine red wine.

Howard and Fran shared a private glance at each other, both being very happy to have spent the evening together with Fran's family. Mr. Dwyer, as was tradition, passed around festively wrapped gifts to all. The Dwyers had even thought to include Howard with a few gifts. They unwrapped their gifts and boxes at each one's own pace, exchanging heartfelt "thank yous" and holding up their prizes with appreciation. As the exchange reached its natural end, Fran opened her last gift; this one from Howard which had been conveniently held in reserve by Mr. Dwyer. The box was large and simply wrapped, obviously the job of a bachelor. However, as Fran opened the box, finding it only filled with red packing tissue, a confused look spread across her face. She stole a glance at Howard as she dug around inside the box, not too dissimilar to a child looking for the prize inside a Cracker Jack's box. While Fran was busy digging, Howard dropped to one knee in front of Fran, who was seated on the couch with her mother, and removed the small blue box with a neat red bow from his suit jacket. A collective pause was shared by all as the realization struck of what was occurring. Fran had said yes, not that her answer was ever really in doubt, and the evening took an even more festive turn.

As expected on any Saturday morning, the Abramenkovs left at the usual time even though it was Christmas morning. Howard led the team that morning, being the most senior of the agents. All other teams were either off or short-handed that morning due to the holiday. Howard kept the team tight, not wanting any repeats of past problems, and the team took the two through their usual paces. Today's journey was typical, albeit shorter due to many stores remaining closed on Christmas morning. The team never lost sight of the Abramenkovs, returning them back to their apartment by early afternoon.

Considered a success on his watch, Howard dismissed the team early that day, as all agreed they had "worked" the entire shift. What no one could have realized was Abramenkov was only out that day as a decoy. While the team was preoccupied with their quarry, a low level female Soviet Mission employee, named Olga Petrova, had made her way by train to Hoboken, New Jersey, to meet Bauer at a neighborhood bakery owned by a German Jewish family who had escaped Nazi Germany shortly after Kristallnacht. It was here that the Nike Rocket plans were returned to Bauer while he purchased a morning strudel for Johan and himself. Bauer had plenty of time to return the plans to his office at the Picatinny Arsenal. After all, it was Christmas morning, and although nearly all employees wouldn't even give the thought of going into work for an hour or two that morning, the limited guard staff would only mark it up to Bauer's eccentricities.

Chapter 45
NYC
February 1952

Jack awoke late, having worked the night shift following Abramenkov. Howard was already awake, on his second cup of coffee, and halfway through The New York Times weekend edition. Howard still marveled at the exhaustive detail of the Sunday edition, reconfirming his knowledge that New York was the epicenter of the universe. "Good morning, Sleepyhead. What time did you call it last night?" Howard asked.

Jack began pouring his first cup of very black coffee from the peculator in their small kitchen, and joined Howard at their small dining table near the balcony French doors. "Must have been just after midnight or so. We had put Abramenkov and the lovely Tatiana to bed at about 2300, and I guess it was about midnight when the light in their bedroom was turned off. It was everything I could do to avoid thinking about that Communist pig giving it to that beautiful creature. I tell you Howard, she deserves much better," Jack said with a wry smile.

"Careful Captain, someone might get the wrong impression that you're a sympathizer," Howard joked. "I have to admit, she does project an exotic sexiness. Kind of reminds me of Veronica Lake," Howard offered. "You must have stopped off for a drink at wherever you've been keeping yourself these past few months. I heard you come in sometime after three this morning."

"Watching me too these days, Howard?" Jack snapped. "Didn't realize you had the detail."

After an uncomfortable pause, Howard spoke. "Jeez, sorry Jack. I was just joking. You're your own man. Didn't mean to pry," Howard offered in a sincere and conciliatory tone. Howard had noted previous outbursts from Jack in the past few months, but had marked it off to long hours and the grind of the job.

Jack turned from the window and the bright morning sun, collecting his thoughts. "No Howard, it's me who is sorry. You didn't deserve that. It's just, you know..." Jack left the sentence unfinished. "Howard, I've been meaning to talk to you about our living arrangements. Listen, with you and Fran making plans to marry this spring, I want you to take the apartment for the two of you."

"I couldn't Jack. This is your place. I can't thank you enough for taking me in and giving me a home away from home. In fact, your friendship and our work together means the world to me, Old Man," Howard offered, using Jack's frequent nickname for Howard. "Fran and I can find our own place. I will start looking soon."

Jack turned to face Howard. "Forget it Howard, my mind is already made up. This place is perfect for you two. Fran can walk to work from here and you're just a couple of No.6 stops away," Jack said, referring to the New York subway's most popular local train line on a north to south, heading straight up the heart of Manhattan. "Besides, I've been spending most of my days up in Midtown anyways. I really won't need a two bedroom anymore after we are no longer cohabitating like two spinster widowers," Jack explained, returning to his usual dry sense of humor. Howard had always liked this most of Jack. His constant ability to never take any situation too seriously, and infuse the mundane to tragic with a sense of wit which had balanced their friendship over the years.

"Ah, Jack, you've really solved a big dilemma for Fran and me. You're right, this place would be perfect for us. And the spare bedroom would allow us the luxury of expanding our little family, if you know what I mean," Howard said with a wide smile.

Jack certainly did know. He had become a bit jealous of Howard and Fran's relationship over these past few months. Jack returned to staring out the window as the steam of his coffee swirled in the bright morning sun. Many things weighed heavily on his mind. True love, would he ever have that experience? Or at least recognize it if it came his way?

Chapter 46
Union Square Station
February 18, 1952

    Howard deployed the team south and not directly on their target this day. He had successfully argued his surveillance theory to SSA Robinson. This didn't happen without incident. Jack, and a few others who had increasingly sided with him as of late, launched "professional" objections. Howard progressively bought into the theory that all agents were not created equal. Jack's latest minions were known as "Little Agents" who could only be trusted with small cases or "Helper Agents" who always volunteered to work on others' cases, but never accomplished much on their own.

    Although still building experience, Howard's work to date had impressed Robinson, who had grown to appreciate his tenacity and analytical mind. Howard's training as a radio operator and education as an engineer had honed his ability to think methodically. Engineers know that the stability of the most gigantic structure depends on the integrity of its smallest element; a failed bolt or a misplaced pin can have huge consequences. Howard approached his investigations like engineering problems, by breaking them down into smaller and more manageable problems. He then identified viable solutions through theory and practice. Others allowed their "gut" feelings to guide their approach. Howard saw nothing wrong with the latter approach, especially when confronted with an imminent threat. However, if you had the luxury of time, breaking a problem down in stages often revealed better solutions.

Howard successfully argued to Robinson that Abramenkov had effectively evaded their surveillance net on numerous occasions. Howard's own experience with losing Abramenkov at the pharmacy in Midtown was an eye opening experience. Howard didn't know that Robinson had placed a lion share of the blame on Jack and not Howard for losing Abramenkov near the pharmacy. So, Howard set out to map Abramenkov's movements and discovered a pattern in his travels on Saturdays. Abramenkov was last seen on several occasions heading towards subway stations that converged on the area around Union Square or points south. Howard proposed to Robinson that the bulk of the team pre-deploy to Union Square and take up static positions at surrounding coffee shops, newspaper stands, and the like. Only one of the team would have to call out Abramenkov and his wife as they departed their apartment. Howard also identified area New York Police Department (NYPD) precincts to use for communications as each had land lines and the Bureau radio system was spotty at best. Most radically, Howard proposed using young female FBI staff to augment the Agents. Howard theorized Abramenkov and other intelligence officers could regularly detect surveillance Agents in certain situations as they didn't reflect the environment. A team comprised of only middle-aged white males wearing suits and fedoras on NYU's campus would clearly stand out. Howard offered that young women would blend in better, and if coupled with the same Agents, would provide sufficient cover. More importantly, Howard suggested to Robinson these same women with proper training could be better at surveillance than men. They all had been chosen for their various positions in the FBI as records clerks, phone operators, and transcriptionists for a reason. They each possessed an uncanny ability to remain focused and displayed a high level of attention to detail. Howard had read about past perception experiments in which females fared better than men at visual recognition clues. And it was obvious to Howard from his relationship with Fran that women could possess gifted analytical minds.

With the plan approved, the team had deployed seamlessly. Howard himself was positioned at a coffee shop on East 14th Street, which provided him a direct line of sight to one of two exits from Union Station. At about half past 9:00 A.M., SA John Calhoun called the 6th Precinct on West 10th Street and notified the team of the Abramenkovs' departure from their residence. By Howard's calculations, the team should be their sharpest at about 10:30 to 11:00 A.M., which would allow Dmitry and Tatiana to enjoy their same cup of coffee at their typical café, before starting their true movement. Howard was convinced that if Dmitry didn't make the surveillance from home to the café and on at least one following cover stop, he would start his true operational run.

Nearly on schedule, at about 10:50 A.M, the Abramenkovs surfaced onto 4th Avenue from the Union Square Station. They walked north on 4th before heading east on East 16th Street. They held hands and stopped to window shop at several store fronts. Howard knew that Dmitry's training included the use of the large reflective windows to check for a tail. The couple appeared like several others out for a late morning stroll on an unusually warm winter's day. But Howard and the team knew better. The team had melded into a well oiled machine, learning to buffer to avoid detection, and to deploy in anticipation of a target's move. In addition, Robinson had bought Howard's theory, and approved the addition of female FBI staff. This allowed the team to set a "picket fence" around the Abramenkovs and avoid walking in concert with the couple. Tailing surveillances were too easy for a trained intelligence officer to detect. For close to an hour, the Abramenkovs squared the neighborhood, taking their time to check for the team, using windows from inside and outside of stores. Before long, the couple entered the Strand bookstore, which was bustling with shoppers both from the surrounding neighborhoods and students from NYU's nearby campus. Near the back of the store, Dmitry and Tatiana split, and Dmitry quickly made his exit. Abramenkov's pace quickened as he headed due west, causing Howard and the others to fight the urge to run after him. All knew that they needed to maintain some space or run the risk of sure detection. Howard signaled to Jack that he was heading ahead of Abramenkov stretching their coverage beyond their ability to effectively communicate the target's location.

Howard was now working on a hunch. He had given a lot of thought to Dmitry's end game, so to speak. Was he responsible for BRAVE or one of the other mysterious agents? For some time now, Howard had identified the NYU campus, with all its highly educated staff and storied programs, as a potentially rich targeting environment for the GRU. This is where Howard had to abandon the numbers and trust his instincts. He knew he was out on a limb as he broke contact with the team. Furthermore, with Jack taking over responsibility for the team, Howard ran the risk of hearing an earful from him and other distracters if his last minute decision ended in disaster.

Howard arrived on the NYU campus well past the last established post in the picket at 11th Street. Howard took up a position within a covered walk area in front of the Main

Building located on the east side of Washington Square, between Washington and Waverly Places. From here, he had a fairly unobstructed view across Washington Square, along with several of the square's ingress and egress spots. After about ten minutes, with still no sign of Abramenkov, Howard grew nervous and moved across the square, to the corner of West 4th and Washington Square South Streets. As he rounded the corner of an unremarkable red brick building, Howard caught a glimpse of Abramenkov up the block and heading north. Howard sprinted at a break neck speed to close the distance, but lost Abramenkov when he turned east on MacDougal Alley.

Howard slowed at the corner and stole a peek, his heart racing with adrenaline. What he saw now was Abramenkov walking at a much slower pace, upright and confident as he held a Saturday Evening Post in his left hand. Howard's spirits, the thrill of being alone and right on Abramenkov immediately took a hit as he sensed, no, knew that whatever Abramenkov had set out to do, he had accomplished. What had Abramenkov done during his moment in the clear? Had he conducted a brush pass, set a signal, cleared a drop? Howard was clueless, and more so, angry. He was angry at himself for failing to account for the NYU campus in his surveillance net. Where Abramenkov succeeded, the team failed. But Howard would not allow anyone else to take the hit on this one. Howard felt utterly defeated, and exhausted by the experience. He had been so close to finally realizing a tangible success, something that often eluded the dedicated counterintelligence professional.

Howard continued to follow Dmitry, giving the latter a large expanse of space. Howard wanted Abramenkov to be convinced that his operation today was without any detection so that he would return to the area again, allowing the FBI to set a trap. The walk back to Union Square was not far measured by distance, but to Howard, it seemed like an eternity. He felt nauseous from the excess of adrenaline now dumping unused into his stomach, and chills coursed through his extremities. Howard approached the team and gave instructions for everyone to stand down. As he explained what he had seen, or more so, what he had not seen, Jack gave Howard a look that could only be taken as disappointment. Something changed between them that day. Howard could not be certain, but their friendship had taken a hit from which it would not recover. Now, to only break the good and bad news to SSA Robinson, was something Howard did not relish.

Chapter 47
NYU Campus
Later that Morning
February 18, 1952

Fran decided to spend the morning in her office grading undergraduate papers as Howard had to work yet another Saturday. Why him and what is so important? Fran thought, not really doubting Howard's work, but more out of frustration for losing another weekend to the FBI. As Fran stepped out of her office to stretch her legs and head to the staff lounge for another cup of coffee, she ran headlong into Dr. Bauer, knocking her to her very firm but now very sore rear end.

"I'm so sorry, my dear", Bauer apologized, but lacking sincerity, as he helped Fran to her feet. "I must really be more careful," Bauer continued.

Fran nodded, but before she could verbally accept Bauer's apology, he was off at a quick pace down the hallway. Odd, Fran thought. What really are the odds that we keep running into each other? Not thinking much more of the incident, she dusted herself off and continued on her way to the lounge.

Chapter 48
New York Office of the FBI
Late Afternoon
February 18, 1952

Howard did not deserve the level of criticism exacted by Jack and the others. He had taken them closer to Abramenkov's activities than any past surveillance. More importantly, he confirmed his theory that the NYU campus could very well be Abramenkov's end game. But who was his agent? Howard wondered, as the others debated for the umpteenth time the morning's events. Howard knew from Fran's work that since the end of the war, NYU had become a sprawling campus filled with researchers and graduate students with access to highly proprietary information, including work on U.S. government contracts. As the others droned in the background, Howard applied his analytical mind to the problem. Howard thought that if he calculated the time frame defined by when Abramenkov was last seen to when he was again acquired, if he ran trial runs fitting within the time frame on the campus to identify ingress and egress points, and overlaid these routes on a campus map, he might be able to identify logical paths Abramenkov could have taken during his operation. At best, Howard knew he could only possibly identify the where and whens, but not the all important who. So how to find the who took over Howard's mind, oblivious to SSA Robinson calling his name.

"Agent Brooks," Robinson called for the third time, bringing Howard back to reality. As Howard's attention was back to the present, he noticed the others at the conference table staring at him. "I think the conversation has focused long enough on the negatives," Robinson continued. "Explain to us how we capitalize on what we did learn today."

"Yes, sir, thank you. Let me first acknowledge to the team that I broke a cardinal rule as team leader by abandoning the net without keeping the team together. SA Larsen and the others all have made valid points, and I take full responsibility for the breakdown in communications. Our efforts today could have resulted in the identification of one of Abramenkov's agents." Even as Howard acknowledged his faults that day, he wondered why Jack, of all people, had become his biggest detractor.

"Howard, let's move forward. I trust that in the future, all protocols will be followed and we will not have a repeat of this situation. Let's turn our focus now to what we learned today and how we will exploit these developments." Howard appreciated Robinson's tact, and knew that he still enjoyed his trust.

"Gentlemen, I believe we now know Abramenkov uses the Union Square area as part of his surveillance detection run. More importantly, I believe he uses the NYU campus to conduct operational activity. This may not explain all of his Saturday activities, but it does give us a great place to start. Additionally, we learned he separates from his wife Tatiana before heading out on his final phase. I've come up with a plan to better identify where his final act takes place," Howard stated before explaining his assessment and laying out the plan to the assembled others.

Back at their shared desk area, Howard and Jack worked in silence. Today's events and recent encounters with

Jack could not be ignored, Howard thought. Their friendship was definitely strained, and possibly irrevocable. They worked in this manner into the early evening, not once exchanging words.

Chapter 49
Howard and Jack's Apartment, NYC
Early Evening
February 18, 1952

Fran offered to clear the dishes as Howard mixed them a Manhattan at the nearby metal and glass stand, an art deco find Howard had acquired at a weekend flea market in Brooklyn. This was the first piece of furniture that he and Fran had technically bought together, and would be one of few remaining articles once Jack moved out the following weekend. When would he find time to shop for more furniture? Operation RED EYE consumed both night and day, one blurring into the next. Fran was the only thing that kept him sane.

Howard returned to the kitchen and took up his familiar station drying the dishes. As he drifted in thought over his relationship with Jack, and the day's events in Union Square, Fran interrupted with a whisper in his ear. "What's on your mind, Pooh?" Fran asked, quietly using her pet name for Howard. Howard had bought Fran a well worn Winnie the Pooh teddy bear at the same Brooklyn flea market, something she cherished dearly.

Howard hesitated before responding. Working for the FBI could be difficult enough, but working counterespionage came with its own inherent challenges. It would be simple if Howard worked bank robberies or organized crime where the office's exploits would often lead the evening radio news bulletins or headline The New York Times. In counterespionage, in Howard's world, you didn't discuss your work with anyone under the cardinal rules of having the appropriate clearances, and more importantly, a need to know. However, Howard and Jack's distancing relationship and recent problems were open conversation with Fran so Howard recounted the day's encounter.

"I had a run in with Jack today. He was very vocal in front of the other guys about my handling of an operation today. Jack's sway and influence over some of the senior team members complicates things for me," Howard said.

"Well, removing you as the focus of his ire, did he have a point? I mean, was he right about how the operation was handled?" Fran asked.

"To a degree, yes", Howard replied. "But his reaction was overly visceral. After all, Robinson had given the team lead to me based on my assessment that we needed to change our approach in order to maximize our chances for success. In my work, success is often measured in small degrees, as major victories are often elusive. You have to work tirelessly and with tenacity to basically put yourself in a position to get lucky. And today, based on my design, we did get lucky. I'm not so much worried about the other members of the team, but Jack, I would have expected a friend to look past some of my errors in judgment and focus on the positives. The bottom line, we are further ahead than we've ever been."

"You two used to be so inseparable, Howard. Maybe it's not work, but something else altogether that's bothering him. Jack just needs to find out how to be happy, and then maybe your friendship will return to normal. People change and this city can take its toll. Not everyone flourishes in this environment, even those born here. Some say it's too many people in too little space," Fran said as she wrapped her arms around Howard and nuzzled her nose in the nape of his neck. "You seem to have adapted well my love, but after all, you have me," Fran said as her bright shining eyes met his. For a moment, all worries passed from Howard.

Chapter 50
Howard and Jack's Apartment, NYC
February 19th, 1952

Howard was on his second cup of coffee when Fran emerged from their bedroom wearing one of his Iowa State boxing club t-shirts and nothing more. Howard knew he could really get used to this. Fran looked beautiful day and night, but especially with her hair tossed and with small lines across the side of her face from the folds in the pillow. Marriage was going to be wonderful.

"Good morning, Babe," Howard said as he poured hot water from the tea kettle into a large China mug. Fran preferred tea, never acquiring the taste for bitter coffee. "What's on the agenda today?"

"Well, it is Sunday, Howard, and I've been a bit neglectful of my good Catholic girl upbringing since I met a handsome and wicked Protestant," Fran teased as she grasped the cup of steeping tea from Howard and kissed him on his cheek. "I really should get to Mass this morning. What would you think about joining me?" Fran asked with a bit of trepidation, not knowing how Howard would respond. The topic of religion had not come up very often, but with their engagement, Fran knew her parents would insist on a traditional Catholic wedding Mass.

"Oh, I think I could handle it, Fran. You don't think I will spontaneously combust when I enter the church, do you?" Howard teased Fran, letting her know she could relax and they could openly discuss the topic. "After all, growing up, I had attended Mass more than a few times with my friend Billy when I stayed overnight with his family in nearby Fort Dodge," Howard continued. "Also, at Framingham during the war, our Army Air Corp Chaplain was Catholic and he would offer universal communion to all of Christian faith."

"Excellent, Pooh," Fran replied with warmth. She was happy to hear that Howard realized marriage would call for personal compromise if they were to make it work.

After mass at Immaculate Conception on 14th Street and a light lunch at a nearby café, Fran told Howard she had to stop by her office at NYU to pick up a few papers. Although a Sunday and a rare day off as of late, Howard offered to accompany Fran, seizing the opportunity to walk the campus and collect data to flesh out his analysis.

Fran led Howard down Washington Place towards Greene Street and stopped at the Brown Building, an old garment factory which was donated in 1929 to NYU by Frederick Brown, a real estate speculator and philanthropist. They continued on Washington Place past Greene and arrived at the Main Building, NYU's oldest original campus building constructed in 1895. Walking a short distance west, they arrived at Washington Square East, which ran north and south, forming the east border of the park. From there, Fran's tour continued to include several stops, such as the loft buildings, concentrated near Washington Square and in proximity to the Main Building. These included Pless Hall, Pless Annex, Goddard, the East Building, and Shimkin Hall. Being a Sunday, there was limited vehicle traffic and the air was surprisingly fresh and mild for this time of year. Howard longed for spring and stretching his legs on a long run.

The tour culminated at the Education Building located on the northwest corner of West Fourth and Greene Streets, and the home of Fran's office. "Be careful Howard," Fran said as they turned the corner in the corridor towards her office. "It can be like crossing 42nd Street at rush hour."

"I don't get it," Howard said oblivious to the reference. "Looks pretty abandoned around here," Howard replied.

"I don't know how many times I've run into Dr. "In-a-Hurry" lately on a weekend. The man appears like a ghost out of nowhere. If you're not careful, he'll run you over, ignorant of fellow pedestrians, or in my case, beautiful PhD candidates," Fran said with a smile as she unlocked her shared office door and turned on the light.

"Who is Doctor, what did you call him? Not any competition for the attention of a beautiful doctor in the making, I hope?" Howard jested.

"Don't be silly. His name is Dr. Bauer, and he's got to be twice my age, Darling. But you do know how I like to be knocked off my feet, literally and figuratively," Fran retorted referencing their fateful encounter on the NYU campus which brought them back together. "You may have met him on our first date at the University reception. Actually, now that I think of it, that's not entirely accurate. I think he almost bowled you over when we entered the reception hall. Odd, right?" Fran asked.

"Sure is. The man must make it a habit to run everywhere he goes. Who is he, by the way?" Howard asked.

"Well, I don't know much about him really. He's an adjunct, meaning, he's part-time faculty, and he lectures one undergraduate class on weekends in my department. I think he is a research scientist at a government facility or the like in New Jersey. I'm not sure which really. He's German for sure and married, I think. At least, I have noticed a ring. But now that I think of it, I've never seen him at any University events with anyone. He did once mention a son during one of our "run-ins" this past Christmas. Why do you ask?" Fran stated as she turned her attention to removing papers from her desk drawer and sorting through them.

"Oh, just being sociable I guess," Howard replied. "I should start to get to know more about your life here on campus since it will soon be even a greater part of my life." But Howard wasn't being entirely truthful in his reply to Fran. He wasn't sure why he cared really, but he never passed up a mystery. Howard's intuitive mind had put himself in a position to get "lucky" on more than one occasion. He had learned during his yet short career with the Bureau that it was always easy to forget unimportant information than never to have possessed it in the first place. "Has he been here at NYU for years?"

"No, must have started sometime in the late 40's, I think. He was not at NYU when I was working on my graduate degree. It was definitely post-war. I don't know if Dr. Bauer falls into this category or not, but many German scientists were brought to the U.S. or to England just before and after Berlin fell. Many worked on secret Nazi government programs, including many in advanced weaponry and rocket science. It's kind of a dirty secret in academia that many of our recent technological advancements are the result of a

German brain drain. The Germans have always been known for their academic focus on the sciences. Johannes Kepler, Max Planck, Werner Von Braun, and of course Dr. Einstein are all great examples. The Nazi government poured a lot of money and time into the sciences leading up to the war. Although the U.S. now leads the world in advanced understanding of nuclear physics, many in academia know that we wouldn't have won the race in the development of the atomic bomb if it weren't for Dr. Einstein immigrating to America. He was visiting the United States when Adolf Hitler came to power in 1933 and did not go back to Germany, where he had been a professor at the Berlin Academy of Sciences. Einstein personally alerted FDR that Germany might be developing an atomic weapon and recommended that the U.S. begin similar research.

Not wanting Fran to know his ulterior motive for wanting to know more about Braun, Howard turned the conversation back to their task at hand and the rest of their Sunday afternoon. But before letting the matter lie, Howard suggested a stroll about campus as it was a "remarkably warm February day." Of course, Howard had other reasons to explore the campus.

Chapter 51
New York Office of the FBI
Morning
February 20, 1952

As Jack had called in sick that day, Howard asked SA Edmond Hurst to help him with some address checks in Brooklyn. Ed was a native of Brooklyn and had served with the 82nd Airborne, seeing action in Sicily and Normandy. Ed's family owned an ethnic German style brauhaus which Howard and Fran had frequented more than once. Ed was a hard working agent, with an even temper and dry wit. Although well over six feet tall and chiseled lean from his airborne training, Ed didn't use his size to impose his will. He chose, instead, to use his sharp intellect and quiet confidence for success. Howard had always liked working with Ed. In fact, these days, he would easily choose working with Ed over Jack. Howard had tired of worrying about his relationship with Jack, and had decided not to focus any more energy on the problem. If their friendship was to survive, only time would tell.

Howard's interrogation of Zhukov had resulted in a list of names and addresses of other CPUSA members and sympathizers. None of these leads had panned out to date beyond a few small catches. Some were even dry holes based on more than one subject moving out of the city. Howard had sent leads to other offices, but had not heard if any resulted in any substantial information. Howard also found that some had renounced membership after eventually maturing and leaving such idealistic pursuits behind in order to focus on providing for growing families. Howard knew he must thoroughly check all if he was to put himself in a position to get lucky, but first he had to meet with Robinson in private.

After Howard had toured the NYU's Washington Square campus with Fran, he devised a plan to set in motion a trap to snare Abramenkov's agent. Something else about that morning tour had struck Howard. Their conversation about Bauer and his background stayed implanted in the recesses of his mind. Was it Bauer's possible work for the Nazi government, or his hurried and distant manner described by Fran? Whatever it was, Howard knew he must internalize these thoughts and revisit them when things were quiet, usually when his mind was supposed to turn off for the day. Howard knocked on Robinson's door.

"Come in," Robinson yelled from inside. As Howard entered, Robinson directed him to one of two chairs opposite his wood and steel desk, minimally adorned with a family photo, a name placard, an ink pad, and a large stamp that could often be heard pounding papers from outside in the bullpen area. Howard took the offered seat and started to outline his plan.

Robinson listened patiently as Howard detailed his ideas on deploying the team at various choke points on the NYU campus. Howard had brought in a map he had obtained from Fran under the auspices of adding it to the FBI's library of records. Next, Howard detailed that the team should not follow Abramenkov to the campus through his normal surveillance detection route as that may only tip him off and cause him to abort his planned operation. Instead, Howard argued the team should only focus its efforts on the campus and allow Abramenkov to walk into the trap. Additionally, Howard advised that the team should only deploy on weekends. Howard stressed that the goal would be to identify the operational activity such as a dead drop, brush pass, or direct agent contact. Then they would either let Abramenkov go as they pursued the contact for identification or continued to survey the drop location for the agent to carry out his part.

    Robinson only interrupted once or twice to clarify team positions and offer realignment suggestions. Howard concurred with Robinson's placements, appreciative of the SSA's experience and guidance. Robinson signed off on the plan and they scheduled the team to work over the next weekend under Howard's team lead.

Chapter 52
Manhattan Terrace Neighborhood, Brooklyn, New York
Afternoon
February 20, 1952

Ed drove as he knew Brooklyn's juxtaposition of odd avenues, streets, and parkways better than Howard. As they turned off of Avenue J and pulled their sedan slowly to the curb in the 1000 Block of East 29th Street, Brooklyn, Ed parked a few houses down the block and on the opposite side of the street from the apartment of Melvin Nowicki. Ed recommended they sit and watch for a while as Manhattan Terrace was a traditional working neighborhood and most men didn't return home until early evening. Nowicki was, in fact, a dock worker working at the Brooklyn Navy Yards. The background compiled on him after receiving the tip from Zhukov indicated he had joined the Worker's Party in the early 1940's, and a bad leg and advancing age had provided him a deferment from service during the war.

As they sat idle with the car to prevent plumes of exhaust telegraphing their two man surveillance, the car grew cold. It was a good thing they had stopped off for some sandwiches and a thermos of coffee. Howard thought an old agent's sage advice about always stopping for a sandwich before shagging a lead was some of the best advice he had ever received. The old agent had told Howard that in this man's organization, no one could be expected to take care of him as well as himself.

One hour turned into the better part of three, but as they grew increasingly weary and the thermos became increasingly empty, Howard noticed a woman walking down the street towards Nowicki's building. It was a typical upper and lower in which the lower was occupied by the building's owner and the upper was converted into either one or two apartments. Nowicki, a widower, became the sole occupant of the upper after his children had grown and moved on to raise their own families. The woman stopped for a moment on the entrance stoop before slowly opening the door and disappearing inside the shared vestibule. Both Howard and Ed assumed she must be Mrs. McKinley, the wife of the building owner and first floor occupant. However, just a moment or two after she had entered, the woman quickly exited, returned to the sidewalk, and walked back the way she had come.

Both Howard and Ed thought the incident odd, and had to make a split decision about either remaining in place as they waited for Nowicki, or following the woman. They exchanged glances, and without a need for words, Howard and Ed exited their car and started after the woman. Three blocks later, they watched her enter the Avenue J station, an elevated New York train station with a direct route through Brooklyn and back into Manhattan. Howard continued after her while Ed headed back to retrieve the car, both agreeing to call into the office to reconnect.

On the train, Howard sat at the opposite end in the car with a copy of The New York Post in an attempt to blend in with the few occupants headed west into the city. The woman, in her mid fifties, sporting a bad blonde hair dye under a paisley head scarf, held her large leather bag tightly to her chest. From her body language, Howard thought her to be a bit nervous and something about her evoked that sixth sense possessed by good agents honed from years of study of the human condition. They rode the train together, but apart, all the way to Grand Central before she made her first exit. The woman exited the large, ornate and expansive station, and chose to meander at a few shops without making any purchases before reentering the station and taking the Number 6 train uptown. While waiting at the platform, Howard called the office to update his progress and learned Ed had returned. Howard told Ed to sit tight and he would check in later.

Exiting at the 86th Street station, Howard gave the woman plenty of room as he was now convinced her movements were indicative of a dry cleaning run commonly deployed by Soviet intelligence. An hour later, as she entered through the side entrance of the Soviet Mission, Howard had confirmation to his and Ed's hunch. For the first time in long time, after many dead ends, Howard basked in the glow of success concerning Zhukov's information. A spurt of energy coursed through his veins reawakening his spirit. Their persistence had finally paid off. Howard was convinced Nowicki was somehow involved with Soviet intelligence. It was time to pay him a direct visit and bring to bear the full weight of the FBI.

Chapter 53
Outside Nowicki's Apartment, Brooklyn, NY
Early morning
February 24, 1952

Howard and Ed had briefed the team late Wednesday afternoon after Howard returned from identifying the woman entering the Soviet Mission. From a photo book compiled with biographies of identified Soviet Officials, they identified their mysterious woman as Olga Petrova, a bookkeeper employed at the Consulate for over three years. As she wasn't a primary target, the FBI hadn't paid her any attention outside of documenting her through photos and logs entering and exiting the Consulate. Today, Friday, was selected as the day to snatch Nowicki as he exited his apartment and headed to the navy yards. SSA Robinson had deployed teams of two, covering all avenues of egress from the apartment house, including the rare rear alleyway.

At about 0530, Nowicki exited the building's shared front door wearing a plaid workman's coat and black watchman's hat. Nowicki, carrying a battered black metal lunch box common for laborers, turned south and began a slow walk, hampered by his bum knee and icy sidewalk. There would be no need today for Howard to run down and tackle anyone. Nowicki presented no resistance upon being confronted by Jack and SA Terrance Garnier, a native of Chicago who had recently transferred in from Omaha. Once patted down for weapons, Howard led Nowicki, his head down and body slump, back to their car. Ed Hurst jumped in as the driver and Garnier climbed in up front. Howard sat in the back with Nowicki, providing him a chance to start the interrogation.

"What is it you want with an old man?" Nowicki protested, but not all that strongly. "You are going to cost me a full day's pay and risk my union card for not calling the foreman."

"Mr. Nowicki, your job is the least of your worries right now. The Internal Security Act of 1950 allows your detention based on the imminent threat of espionage or sabotage. You should be more concerned about a life in prison right now."

"I don't know what you are talking about!" Nowicki viscerally protested with genuine concern in his voice. "I'm an old man and a threat to no one. This is a big mistake I tell you."

"No mistake, Mr. Nowicki," Howard continued in a calm voice, free of menace, a tactic purposely chosen by Howard so he could become Nowicki's confessor. "We have been aware for some time now of your membership in the Worker's Party and CPUSA. Most of the time, we wouldn't be overly concerned, however, recent events have brought us here today. Your actions are, indeed, at the heart of why you are sitting in the back of this government car and heading to our office in Manhattan. You should think long and hard about why you brought us here today. Think it over, Mr. Nowicki, while you enjoy the comfort of this warm car."

Howard had designed his interrogation to include the long car ride back into the city. He wanted Nowicki to come to a rather false realization that the FBI knew all about his relationship with Ms. Petrova, which was a bit of a stretch.

The FBI did know there was a connection between Petrova and the address, and they could reasonably extrapolate that Nowicki was involved, based on his affiliations with the Communist groups. However, without a long and time consuming investigation, the McKinleys were as much a consideration as Nowicki himself, as Petrova could have entered either apartment from the shared vestibule outside of Howard and Ed's view.

About one hour later, the FBI team arrived in unison back at the office. Howard had Ed and Terrence escort Nowicki upstairs to an interrogation room while he took his time making a pot of coffee. Howard had asked the team to defer any of Nowicki's questions until Howard returned, again part of his plan to become Nowicki's benevolent confessor. Nowicki's own silence and slumped shoulders confirmed he knew why the FBI wanted to talk to him. It would be up to Howard to extract the nature of Nowicki's relationship with Petrova, and determine how deep was his involvement with Soviet intelligence.

Howard entered the room carrying three cups of steaming coffee and placed one each in front of Nowicki and Ed. Howard held the third and remained standing. Nowicki eagerly grabbed the cup, and without concern for the inside of his mouth, he gulped about half of the cup before setting it down purposefully and looking up at Howard. "What is it you want from me? I've done nothing wrong, and I haven't even attended any of those meetings for years. I was young, stupid, and caught up in the wave of excitement and promise of an equal future. They promised better wages and protection from men working for the bosses," Nowicki said. After a pause, Nowicki continued but with less vigor and protest.

"But it didn't take long to realize these groups were just used by other men who wanted to grab power for themselves. Just like the union bosses, they are more about taking care of themselves than their workers. They use the young idealist as tools to their own wealth and access. I make no apologies because I was my own man and willingly chose my own path. Yes, I believed that Communism could be good for all men, but I learned that men corrupted it just like any other system."

Howard sat down pulling his chair close to Nowicki, close enough to easily touch him if he chose. Nothing separated the two men but a few inches. "No one is here to pass judgment on your internal struggles, Mr. Nowicki. Before today, I should have meant nothing to you in the bigger scheme of life. I'm not your father, your brother, or your clergy," Howard declared, looking Nowicki directly in the eye. After a slight pause to let his statement sink in, Howard continued. "What I am, Mr. Nowicki, is your one and only chance. I am the one and only person who will collect your story and accurately record your own words. This is your one chance to talk openly and honestly. This is your one chance to finally tell someone your suspicions, those things that have been bothering you down to your very soul, those things that you are ashamed of, Mr. Nowicki. I won't pass judgment on you, I will only tell your story in your own words. You can trust me on that, Mr. Nowicki," Howard said in a calm and soothing voice, pausing to let the gravity of the situation set in.

Like a man of the cloth standing before his congregation, delivering a message full of fire and brimstone to an attentive audience, Howard raised the tone and tempo of his voice, exuding urgency. "So, Mr. Nowicki, what is it that you have been thinking about since we last talked in the car and you went silent? What is it that has bothered you for some time now which you feel compelled to get off your chest? What is it you are hiding from your family? What are you ashamed of? This is your one chance, Mr. Nowicki. You may not find the next person you talk with to be so agreeable," Howard finished, hitting a crescendo.

Nowicki's body slumped in submission and his chin fell to his chest. Howard leaned in ever so slightly, and gently placed his hand on Mr. Nowicki's now slightly trembling arm. It was not only as an act of intimacy to complete his role as the confessor, but also an attempt to stop the white China mug from rattling on the room's lone wooden table. Slowly, Nowicki raised his head and brought his eyes to meet Howard's. "This... this is about the woman, isn't it?" Nowicki stammered, just above a hushed tone barely audible to Howard and clearly not loud enough for Ed to hear.

"Yes, it is. Tell me from the beginning, Mr. Nowicki. Don't assume anything. Remember, your honesty may be your savior."

With that, Nowicki gradually came around both physically and emotionally. He slowly regained his voice as he recounted their first meeting the summer before in Brooklyn at a beer hall frequented by dock workers before and after their shifts. She appeared one late afternoon carrying a grocery bag full of mild sausages and crusty bread. She had sat down at a table alone, checking the wall clock from time to time. Nowicki had recognized her from the train he took most days from home to the docks. He thought her to be a handsome woman with the right amount of extra weight which was good for cold nights. Nowicki, having become a widower more than ten years prior, watched her from his own lone table. At first, fifteen minutes and then the better part of a half-hour had past. She looked a bit distraught and appeared as though someone had not shown as planned. Nowicki took a chance. He ordered a second beer for her, one for himself, of course, and then delivered hers personally. She had a kind smile and wasn't put off by his advance. She said her name was Katia and was a widow herself, having lost both her husband and only son to the Great Patriotic War, as the Soviets called the Second World War. She had immigrated to the U.S. and lived with her cousin's family in Brighton Beach. She was supposed to meet someone, Nowicki couldn't remember who, and had to leave soon or the sausages would spoil. Nowicki had a better idea, and before long, she was in his kitchen, cooking the best home meal he had experienced in ages; and later, she was in his bed, where no one had been since he lost his lovely Isabela. Their relationship was one of convenience and need for both of them, or so he thought. They enjoyed each other's company but lived apart due to appearances and her vague explanations of living a complicated life. At first, he saw her two to three times per week, but over the last few months, the frequency of their meals and coupling waned to once every couple of weeks. As the months passed, Nowicki started to notice anomalies in her story and excuses for showing late or not showing at all, the latter becoming the norm. Nowicki didn't mind, as any company at his age was to be desired. However, he thought it peculiar when she requested to have mail delivered to his care and address. Olga explained that her cousin's husband was overbearing and suspicious of his wife's wandering eye. So in order to prevent her cousin trouble, she needed to have personal correspondence and deliveries mailed to Nowicki's address. He thought it a small price to pay for her company and didn't further question the situation. One day, he had come home early to grab a few hours of sleep before covering an extra overnight shift. Nowicki found Olga exiting the vestibule and carrying a small package. She appeared startled by his presence, and nervously explained that she didn't have time to come by later when he was home. He didn't mind really, but just thought it odd. An even stranger occurrence was that one letter had been sent from Western Europe, possibly Vienna, and Olga had appeared that very same day to retrieve it. It was almost as though she was watching for it daily.

When asked by Howard and Ed if he remembered more about the postmark, Nowicki couldn't provide more details. He did, however, tell Howard and Ed that most of the letters for Katia were usually post marked from Jersey City.

Chapter 54
NYU Campus, NYC
Early Saturday Morning
February 25, 1952

The net to catch Abramenkov's agent was set. Howard deployed the team, including Jack, Ed, and Terry at various NYU buildings and public spaces. Their goal was to use vestibules, entry ways, and cafes as concealment as they each covered a specific area of responsibility. If done properly, communication between the team would be minimal. Robinson didn't bat an eye when Howard again asked to deploy the female office staffers as part of the net. These women could not only provide an extra pair of expert eyes, but also provide cover for the team's agents allowing them to fit into the environment on a Saturday. Howard believed couples would be less alerting to Abramenkov, especially when static in public places for an extended period.

The morning was clear and crisp and the team deployed as planned. Unfortunately, Abramenkov and his wife Tatiana never materialized. Jack never called from his position as a lookout near the Abramenkovs' apartment indicating the targets were underway that Saturday, and the team never detected their presence on campus. Howard was bothered of course, bothered that the expended resources didn't pay off. But more so, Howard was disappointed in Jack's choice to volunteer for the lookout assignment rather than deploy with the team on campus. Howard took this as another clear sign of their waning personal and professional relationship. It had deteriorated so far that Jack was now avoiding contact with Howard all together.

Two more Saturdays would come and go without success. On the previous Saturdays, the Abramenkovs followed their usual pattern of coffee and window shopping before disappearing in the breeze. Without the team assigned to take them from their apartment, Jack, the sole lookout, could not keep up and transition with the Abramenkovs during their maneuvers. The risk, of course, was that the Abramenkovs could be conducting unfettered operations without surveillance assigned. Risk versus reward was always at issue. When you're correct, you look like a genius, and when not, you look like a chump. Whether real or imagined, Howard believed Robinson was becoming disillusioned with Howard's plan and his patience was waning. Howard was also certain Fran was becoming a bit frustrated with only having him to herself on Sundays.

They say patience is a virtue. Whether true or not, the team's fourth successive Saturday deployment finally paid off. Jack was not around to celebrate with the rest of the team. He was sent to Washington the previous week to deliver the volumes of surveillance logs and analytical reports developed on the GRU's movements in New York to SSA Lamphere. Similar trips had been made since New York was originally briefed on the Verona reporting concerning KORN, MORSE, and BRAVE. All the more perplexing to Howard, Jack volunteered to make the trip, usually reserved for junior agents.

At about 0900, the lookout alerted the team that the Abramenkovs were on the move. At about 1030, Howard squirreled himself away in a NYU café, popular with both staff and students alike. The café's location on Washington Place and Greene Street placed Howard toward the eastern edge of their deployment perimeter. Other team members were positioned at cross streets every block. The perimeter was defined by Mercer Street to the east, MacDougal Avenue to the west, West 8th Street to the north, and West 3rd Street to the south.

Howard found sitting in a warm café with a bottomless carafe of coffee very civilized compared to sitting on a Washington Square park bench in the chill of the lingering winter. Howard had personally assumed that post the two previous Saturdays for hours at end. Feeling the cold creeping into his bones, Howard's thoughts would drift off to his winter missions aboard the Liberty Belle. Even with the leather flight suits with plug-in electrical heating, the cold would find its way in and drain Howard of his energy. Howard also found sitting on the cold bench with the anticipation of action and adrenalin dumps eerily similar to flight missions; except, of course, for the foreboding presence of death lingering in the atmosphere. There were also the young coeds walking to and fro, often trying to catch Howard's eye. Unfortunately for them, only Fran could hold Howard's attention.

As Howard sat drinking his umpteenth cup of coffee and conducting his third or fourth re-read of The New York Times, after having already mastered the crossword puzzle, he sensed movement different from the normal pulse of the café's patrons. Howard slowly raised his eyes from the Times, and first noted the fast gait of the male subject as he broke the plane of the entry door and briskly walked through the narrow passage between tables and counter stools. As the subject blew by, Howard stole a quick glance and thought he recognized the man. Needing to get a better look at the man's face, Howard counted to one hundred to both slow his pulse and give the man time to settle in. At the count of one hundred, Howard rose and headed for the men's room at the rear of the café. At the last booth, he found Bauer sitting by himself and looking at a worn and tattered paper menu. Bauer appeared oblivious to Howard's presence; and after the appropriate amount of time, Howard made a command decision. He returned to his table, collected his overcoat and fedora, covered his bill, and made for the exit.

Howard knew that his actions in the next few minutes would be crucial to closing the net. He walked east across Greene Street and north across Washington Place to take up a position diagonally from the café. Howard was sure his movements were viewed by both Hurst to the north and Garnier to the south; alerting them something was happening and raising their awareness. About twenty minutes later as the clock was to strike noon, Hurst walked from east to west across Greene Street at Waverly Place. Hurst had not worn his suit and Fedora that day, choosing the look of a tired laborer instead. As he crossed the street, Hurst briefly removed his watch cap and ran his fingers through his hair, alerting team members in sight that Abramenkov had been seen inside the perimeter. Howard had seen Hurst's move and could only smile as he thought both of the possibilities of this being the day they would snare Abramenkov, and also of a Yankees' third base coach signaling a hit away sign to Yogi Bera.

Howard saw both Abramenkov and Tatiana enter the same café Howard and Bauer had chosen that Saturday morning. Through the café's large rectangular windows,

Howard could see Tatiana pause to look at a menu while Dmitry continued towards the back of the café and its restrooms. What Howard had missed by tunneling his attention solely on the Abramenkovs was Bauer's move towards the same restroom. A slight feeling of panic began to replace the chill in Howard's body and a small amount of bile began to rise in his throat. Damn, thought Howard, relax and focus, he told himself.

What seemed like hours, was in reality, moments as time slowed and clarity of thought and vision returned to Howard. Not long after Abramenkov disappeared from Howard's sight line, Bauer exited the men's room and headed for the exit, only momentarily pausing and returning to his table to pay the bill. Howard could see the distaste spreading across the face of the young waitress as she collected her pittance of a tip.

Bauer's signature fast gait was evident as he quickly exited the café and headed west towards Washington Square East. Howard signaled to Hurst to head west on Waverly Place, and Garnier to head west on West 4th Street. At Washington Square East, Hurst picked up Bauer heading north towards his position. From there, the team had an easy time following Bauer to his short visit to the NYU adjunct office, and his commute home via Penn Station. It was Hurst who identified Bauer's residence in West Orange, NJ.

The team had done it and Howard had led them to their prize. Collectively, hundreds of hours of man power, theories debunked and proven, missed holiday and family time, and strained relationships had resulted in an extraordinary victory. More importantly, the FBI was now on a clear and unstoppable trajectory towards snaring an agent and foiling its main enemy in what would later become popularly known as the Cold War.

Chapter 55
New York Office of the FBI
Monday - March 17, 1952 and following weeks

The celebration only lasted through that fateful Saturday evening. Upon returning to the office, Howard revealed his suspicions of Bauer. Sunday was consumed by strategy and collegial arguments over the next steps, and cable traffic between FBIHQ and the NYO. Director Hoover himself became personally involved, something he did quite often when detecting an opportunity for self-aggrandizing and further securing his power over the burgeoning U.S. intelligence machine and its start up agencies. Born out as the Office of Strategic Services (OSS), which had coordinated intelligence activities against the Axis Powers during World War II, the CIA was formally created through the National Security Act of 1947. Hoover could never get over the FBI losing its own foreign intelligence apparatus, the Special Intelligence Service (SIS), which operated in South America during the war and was headquartered in New York. Hoover would never again allow an outside agency to meddle in his affairs, nor would he let the President and his cabinet forget who he was and why he was relevant.

Robinson, Howard, and the rest of the team couldn't be bothered with such political maneuvering, as they were focused on the real work at hand. After the events of Saturday, Howard briefed the team on what he knew about Bauer from Fran, including his work at NYU and the possibility he had come to the U.S. after capture by Allied forces during

WWII. The fact that Howard already knew some information on Bauer allowed the FBI to quickly gain speed. They had yet to learn of his full-time gainful employment at Picatinny, but that knowledge would come in due time.

The team was expanded to include agents who had been assigned to other counterintelligence threat issues of lower priority. Most importantly, Howard was named team lead in principal with overall responsibility as the primary case agent. He requested Hurst be added as his second, as their relationship of trust and friendship had easily developed over the last few months. Robinson assigned Jack to be in charge of the surveillance teams and schedule, which normally would be assigned to a more junior agent and beneath the working of a senior agent such as Jack. However, Jack accepted the assignment without much discussion or fight. Howard suspected Jack saw an opportunity to further distance himself from their now broken relationship. Was it his success in the office or his finding true love with Fran that caused the riff? Howard couldn't quite place it, and fortunately, he had little time to dwell on the issue as long days followed by long nights became the norm.

Howard and Hurst set about building a dossier on Bauer. Hour upon hour was spent investigating his life before and after immigration, his position and access while working for the U.S. government, his position and access at Picatinny, and detailing his current work and social contacts. What they found was a highly educated and intellectual man, who appeared to have lost part of his family to the war, who was respected in his current career field, and who appeared to be a doting father to his son. They also found a man considered to be a relative loner with few, if any, developed personal relationships. Surveillance records reflected he had no current love life even though he was a relative catch based on pedigree and appearance. Outside of time spent with his son, who was by all appearances well adjusted and immersed in the American way of life, Bauer spent his time alone at home with frequent trips to the NYU campus, supposedly to prepare for his class.

Howard and Hurst turned their focus to what Abramenkov and the GRU wanted from Bauer. Intercepts of the letters sent to the dead letter box at Nowicki's apartment in Brooklyn only telegraphed potential meeting times for BRAVE, and included very little in the way of personal needs. The only mention of payment for services was in reference to money needed to pay for college, presumably for Bauer's son Johan. Howard had to be careful in probing Bauer's work at Picatinny to avoid any undue exposure to the investigation. The FBI used records obtained from regular security reviews at Picatinny conducted to maintain government clearances and contracts. Bauer appeared to be a leading researcher on rocket propulsion systems, continuing the work he had started before the war while employed by the German state. Picatinny had received the contract to develop the missile system, America's intercontinental ballistic missile deterrent. This was a highly classified project, and Bauer's possible work on it was very disconcerting.

Chapter 56
New York Office of the FBI
June 1952

June was a glorious month for several reasons; the dreary days of winter and a wet, unpredictable spring had passed, and the warmth of a coming summer had finally taken its hold. Once again, the city was fresh and vibrant. The investigation of Bauer as BRAVE had progressed reasonably well and evidence was building. Most importantly, June brought the most wonderful of days... Fran and Howard's wedding.

They had opted for a relatively intimate affair with family and friends. Howard's parents William and Madge, as well as his siblings attended. Howard's brother Clarence and his wife Evelyn, his sister Edith and her husband Carl, and his sister Gwen and her new husband Roger, all made the trip to New York City by way of train and bus. They were awed by the sheer size and liveliness of America's greatest city. Fran's parents had put up the Brooks family in their spacious home in Brooklyn, and seemed unfazed by the endless comments and questions about life in New York. The Brooks and Dywer men got on exceptionally well considering the vast differences in occupation and lifestyles; and the Catholic/Protestant "issue" didn't seem to get in the way. Howard's mother Madge was just happy that Howard's big day would be celebrated before the eyes of God and not a Justice of the Peace, as Howard and Fran had briefly considered. The Brooks and Dywers would have none of that.

For the honeymoon, the Dwyers treated Fran and Howard to an all expense paid trip to Washington, DC to take in the wonders and sites of our nation's capitol. Howard and Fran stayed at the Mayflower Hotel, once glimpsing Director Hoover lunching at his usual spot in the lobby café. They learned from the concierge that Suite 776, their lovers' getaway for the week, was the same room in which Franklin Roosevelt had lived during his pre-inaugural period, and from which he dictated his famous, "We have nothing to fear but fear itself" speech. They toured the National Mall and all it had to offer, and dined at select hotspots such as the Old Ebbitt Grill and the Occidental Grill. Of course, most nights were busy with extracurricular activities often enjoyed and indulged by newlyweds. Fran and Howard were truly in love, and leisurely spent their time away from the hassles and rat race of their daily lives in New York City.

Fran even indulged Howard as he spent one afternoon at FBIHQ, meeting with SSA Lamphere and Associate Director Clyde Tolson over progress in the BRAVE investigation. Howard learned from Lamphere about Bauer's work in Nazi Germany and his later involvement in the Project Paperclip program which brought German scientists to the U.S. to fast track the government's rocket and weaponry development. According to the reports, Bauer's involvement in the Nazi Party was either never confirmed, or all together whitewashed in order to allow his entry into the U.S. However, Lamphere explained that thorough searches of Bauer's government and wartime records did not reveal much information about his family. The records were sketchy at best, and provided limited information about his family. Bauer's marriage records to Hanna Kirsch were found, as well as birth certificates for a daughter named Gisela and a son named Johan. Missing were any records about the fate of the wife and daughter, but as Lamphere explained, such records in the fading days of the European campaign were not as well maintained by the German government. What was most disturbing, of course, was Bauer's current position at the Picatinny Arsenal, and his classified work on several projects. Tolson's brief attendance at the meeting was to reinforce Director Hoover's personal attention on this matter and his demand that the BRAVE investigation be resolved without delay. Hoover wanted to send the Soviets a clear message that their intelligence and godless activities on American soil, or for that matter anywhere America held interests, would not be tolerated and would be disrupted without impunity.

It was absolutely clear to Howard that this would be the most important case of his life and that his career in the FBI was heavily dependent on a successful outcome. It was also clear to Howard, through his discussions with Lamphere, that his skills and tenacity did not go unnoticed by the FBIHQ executive management. There was some talk of Howard taking a supervisory position at FBIHQ once they had wrapped the BRAVE investigation and affected Bauer's arrest. Howard's career was on the fast track and nothing could interrupt his progress.

Upon returning to New York, Jack had vacated their shared apartment as planned. Jack had left behind a housewarming and wedding gift, a beautiful set of silverware engraved with the loving couple's names and wedding date. The moment was bittersweet for Howard, both a reminder of the close friendship they once enjoyed but also that Jack had officially removed himself from Howard's life.

Chapter 57
New York Office of the FBI
Late Summer Into Early Fall 1952

Upon returning to New York, Howard delivered Hoover's message to SSA Robinson, who in turn briefed Assistant Director in Charge Edward Scheidt. All understood that resources and efforts would double on the BRAVE investigation. What they lacked was evidence. A successful prosecution could not be built on mere suspicion. Yes, it was clear Bauer was BRAVE, but the FBI had no information on what exactly had been compromised.

A plan was set in motion to limit surveillance coverage on Abramenkov in order to encourage his operational activity. However, a fine line had to be walked because if Abramenkov saw too little of his minders, he would question what had changed. The GRU would naturally suspect a compromise in the methodologies or sources. To this extent, and knowing Abramenkov's pattern of servicing BRAVE on Saturdays, the team managed to "lose" their prey more often than not. In its place, the team spent much of its time over the next couple of months focused on Bauer's movements.

On one early Saturday morning, after Bauer had ostensibly arrived early on campus to prepare his teaching plan for his undergraduate Physics Theory course, Bauer paused to tie his right shoe near a low brick wall just east of 5th Avenue on Washington Square North. The wall, which was under repair, separated the small gardens in front of the old row houses. Fortunately for the FBI, Bauer was not a fully trained intelligence officer and his tradecraft was rather sloppy. Hurst and Garnier led the detail that morning and both witnessed Bauer "discard" a brown paper bag from his morning coffee purchased at a neighborhood vendor's cart. As Bauer started to head back towards the Adjunct office, he paused long enough to light an unfiltered cigarette, and somewhat surprisingly well, mark a horizontal line in chalk on a post box on the opposite corner.

As part of the team followed Bauer out of the area and sight of his dead drop, the rest set up a defensive posture around the immediate area. Hurst sat on the short wall long enough to retrieve the bag, take a quick inventory of its contents, and replace the bag with more care than afforded by Bauer. The bag contained a paper napkin with crude writing scribbled on the back. The note simply read, "No progress. Need more time. Will try again at the regular interval."

Hurst immediately phoned the office about the development. Howard, at the recommendation of Robinson, had been removed from the surveillance details in order to concentrate on the big picture. Alice Kenney, a young and vibrant secretary from Staten Island, called Howard at home. Howard immediately made a bee line for the office, and once there, made contact with the team sitting on Abramenkov's apartment. Howard learned that Dmitry and Tatiana had already surfaced at their usual Saturday morning sidewalk café for coffee and a leisurely read of The New York Times. Howard instructed the team to stick with Abramenkov through at least one or two operation moves before conveniently losing him.

The plan paid off as the Abramenkovs arrived on the NYU set late morning as expected. They again visited the Strand Bookstore where Tatiana bought a rather obscure and used book by Valentin Nikolaevich Voloshinov, "Marxism and the Philosophy of Language," and took an early lunch at a local diner frequented by both students and office workers alike. After lunch, they strolled as lovers through Washington Park, which to the team, appeared very natural for the two. By design, their route from the diner to the park took them pass the post box where the chalk mark was clearly legible under taped flyers advertising an upcoming poetry read at the park. At the park, and to the casual observations of others out on an Indian summer day, they appeared to leisurely feed the pigeons. To the team who had been following the Abramenkovs for the better part of a year, and had developed a keen sense of their personality traits and mannerisms, Abramenkov's alertness was slightly elevated, whereas Tatiana's was hyper sensitive.

After about twenty minutes, the Abramenkovs moved in the direction of the garden wall, and as Abramenkov consulted a map of lower Manhattan, Tatiana reached over the wall and retrieved the bag. A fleeting moment was all it took to deposit the crumpled paper bag into her purse, and having apparently got their bearings, the two walked away, back towards the area of Union Square. They did not stop to eat or drink or leisurely shop through windows, but instead, proceeded in a direct route at a quickened pace to the subway. A couple of local stops later and they were deposited back by their apartment. If only Howard and the others could be a fly on the wall and see Abramenkov's agitated state as he burned the diner receipt and slumped in his chair. Not even a shoulder rub and a vodka gimlet delivered by the lovely Tatiana could relieve his distress.

Chapter 58
New York Office of the FBI
Late Fall 1952

Howard's elation over catching Bauer in the act was tempered by complete dissolution of his and Jack's relationship. Victories in counterespionage are difficult to come by and careers can be made when they are attached to high profile cases. The BRAVE investigation was just that, but yet Howard felt emptiness for not being able to celebrate and share the victory with his once closest friend. Furthermore, the prospects of repairing, or at least salvaging, a scrap of their friendship were further complicated by Jack's request to be transferred to FBIHQ. Although a natural career progression for someone with Jack's experience, Howard could only think that part of Jack's motivation was to further distance himself from Howard and the investigation. Howard was certain their strained relationship had reached the point where the two could not work together. Howard also sensed jealousy on Jack's part. Where Howard had once been the protégé, he was now becoming the master. Howard was a natural, with an internal drive to serve his country to the best of his abilities. Howard took his oath to the Constitution and his country's citizenry very seriously. Nothing, including a friendship with Jack, would diminish his passion. In the end, Howard understood he couldn't reverse the tide and important work lay ahead.

Howard received clearance from FBI Headquarters to approach Picatinny officials to determine Bauer's access and identify the projects he had been involved in since arriving in

New Jersey. Not knowing where allegiances would fall amongst researches and academics at Picatinny, Howard knew that the matter would have to be handled with a certain amount of delicacy to prevent exposing their investigation to Bauer.

"Mr. Johnson, my name is Special Agent Howard Brooks and this is Special Agent Hurst. Thanks for taking the time to meet with us at your home and not at your office," Howard offered as they stood at the door of Albert Johnson's suburban New Jersey home on a bright Indian summer Saturday morning. Johnson was a mid-level manager and researcher the FBI had determined would have oversight over Bauer's work at Picatinny. He had also served his country with distinction during the war, obtaining the rank of Colonel.

"This is a bit unorthodox gentlemen, but please do come in. May I offer you two a cup of coffee?" Johnson asked as his wife Erma stood at the threshold between the kitchen and living room.

"Yes, thank you. I'd never turn down an offer for a good cup of strong coffee, Mr. Johnson," Howard quipped as he smiled towards Mrs. Johnson. "Mr. Johnson, what we are about to discuss is highly sensitive and involves classified matters at the arsenal. I assure you we have the appropriate clearances, but I would implore you to contact Associate Director Clyde Tolson in Washington if you have any concerns. Mr. Tolson has personal knowledge of this investigation and he can verify our credentials and authorities."

"I don't believe that will be necessary, Agents Brooks and Hurst. I called an old Army buddy of my mine who is now with the Department of Justice and confirmed your employment," Johnson advised. "How can I help you?"

Mrs. Johnson entered the room and Howard paused long enough to accept the offered cup. Waiting for her to exit and close the door, Howard continued. "Mr. Johnson, what we are about to discuss needs to be kept to yourself and involves matters of national security. We ask that you don't talk to anyone at Picatinny about our conversation, and the reasons will become abundantly clear," Howard paused for effect. "We have reason to believe one or more classified projects at Picatinny have been compromised and provided to a foreign power. We have focused our investigation on one particular employee and we believe you can provide direct insight into this subject's work and access."

"Agents Brooks and Hurst, you have just confirmed every government researcher and patriot's worst fear. I will do anything I can to assist you. Please continue," Johnson replied.

"Mr. Johnson, please share with us what you know about Wilhelm Bauer, including his work at the arsenal and his personal home life. All details are welcome, no matter how small or insignificant you may think. Please let us decide what is important or not," Howard continued, noting Johnson visibly slumped in his chair at the revelation of Bauer's name.

Johnson started talking and didn't stop for nearly two hours, except for questions by Howard and Ed to solicit specific details or to redirect Johnson on certain facts. Johnson started by describing Bauer's detachment from the social network developed amongst fellow researchers, born from long hours in the lab and academic collaboration. He also expressed personal concerns over his background, or lack thereof. Johnson and others in the lab were uneasy from the beginning about Bauer and the circumstances behind his immigration from Germany. However, none could argue that he wasn't a brilliant engineer. What Johnson revealed confirmed the FBI's worst fears. Bauer's past and current work included highly sensitive and cutting edge projects that would greatly compromise our nation's security if the Russians had stolen their designs and capabilities.

  In 1949, the Picatinny Arsenal was tasked to create an artillery piece and shell capable of carrying a nuclear payload. The M65 "Atomic Cannon," the Army's largest artillery gun, was capable of firing both conventional and atomic warheads. The road-transportable cannon was based on the design of the German K5 Railroad Gun, with the goal of giving the U.S. land forces a tactical atomic capability. The project's design team was headed by Robert Schwartz, who assembled a staff to carry out the three-year development effort on what they nicknamed Atomic Annie. Bauer was part of Schwartz's staff, albeit he made little impact. Mainly, he contributed his knowledge of the German rail gun system. Nonetheless, this work on the weapon gave him unfettered access. Johnson advised that after Picatinny completed the final design earlier in 1952, the Pentagon tasked the Watervliet Arsenal in New York for production. He added that the shell was scheduled to be tested sometime in 1953. Beyond the atomic gun, Bauer had contributed to, and therefore had access, to several other classified projects, any of which would set the arms race back years if compromised.

Chapter 59
Howard and Fran's Apartment, NYC
Late Fall 1952

Howard awoke later than usual for a Sunday morning. The BRAVE investigation had become all consuming, mentally as well as physically. He was now regularly working Saturdays in addition to his usual long weeks, and he and Fran's time together had become increasingly short.

"Good morning, Babe," Howard said through a yawn followed by a long stretch. "Why didn't you wake me? Wow, is that really the time?" Howard asked as he cleared early morning gunk from the corner of his eyes and strained to look at the grandfather clock, a wedding gift from Fran's parents.

"Well, Darling, you hadn't been sleeping much as of late, and I couldn't bring myself to rouse you from your bliss. By the way, can you be held liable for secrets spilled in your sleep?" Fran asked as she raised a cup of coffee to her lips hiding the smile forming on her mouth.

"What? What did I say? Did I mention names?" Howard stammered in building panic.

"Don't be silly, Darling, I was only kidding. Here, have a cup of coffee and wake up," Fran replied with now an obvious and mischievous smile on her face. Fran really wasn't kidding, Howard had talked in his sleep, repeatedly mumbling the word "BRAVE."

"Got me," Howard said as he emptied the percolator's grounds and started another pot of coffee.

"I had coffee with Alice yesterday morning to catch up on your office gossip. She told me about Jack's promotion to Washington," Fran said with a bit of trepidation. Fran had been wary of mentioning Jack around Howard as of late, as he apparently had enough on his mind already.

"Yeah, not all that much of a surprise really. Jack has made quite a name for himself over these past few years and it was only a matter of time before he was forced to go. But I can't help but think the timing has something to do with our work together on a major case. Besides, maybe the move is what he needs to lift him out of the increasing malaise he has fallen into. So, I guess that is it for us, at least for a while. He even turned down Robinson's offer for a party before transferring, and he's taking much less time than what policy offers for the transfer transition. It is almost as though he's running from something," Howard explained as he stared blankly out the kitchen window with the steam of a fresh brewed coffee and the low angle of a bright morning sun warming his face.

"Well, Darling, not much you can do now but give it time," Fran said as she walked up behind Howard and nuzzled her nose into the back of his neck.

They stood that way for a few moments without words or a need for any. Fran broke the moment with a few simple words. "Howard, you're going to be a father."

Chapter 60
New York Office of the FBI
Late Fall 1952

Howard was still feeling high and walking on clouds from Fran's news when SSA Robinson called the meeting to order. After the interview with Albert Johnson the previous week, Howard was directed to formulate an action plan to snare Bauer in a trap, and collect enough evidence to secure an indictment from the U.S. Attorney's Office in New York. They needed the case to be airtight based on Bauer's former work for the U.S. Government and to provide the Department of State the necessary ammunition to revoke Abramenkov's Visa, the kiss of death for an intelligence officer posted under diplomatic cover. Howard laid out his plan.

The FBI would first have to secure the cooperation of the arsenal's director. Johnson assured Howard that wouldn't be a problem as the director was a true patriot who had lost his two sons to the war. He would be utterly furious that their research and development may have been compromised and lost to the enemy, especially at the hands of a man whose country had robbed him of watching his boys further mature and become fathers themselves. Howard proposed assigning Bauer to a new project, false in design and application, and Johnson had the perfect solution.

The U.S. Government had conceived for years the concept of launching an earth satellite vehicle for communications into the earth's orbit. Project proposals to design a rocket propulsion system capable of delivering such a platform had yet to be assigned to any particular research facility as current technologies were years away from fruition. However, the concept was common knowledge in the research community as America was beginning to enter the space race. New staged delivery systems, command and control systems, and fuels would have to be developed. Johnson suggested that he personally oversee the "new" project with Bauer and others working part-time. Bauer would not be suspicious, as his expertise in rocket systems would make it logical for him to be assigned to the project.

The rest of Howard's proposal was fairly straight forward. The new project would be the right bait to entice Bauer to steal development plans and deliver them to Abramenkov. The team would focus on Bauer's movements, and surveillance assignments were laid out to provide twenty-four hour coverage. Special care would need to be taken to prevent Bauer from detecting the team. Properties providing a direct view of Bauer's residence and Picatinny's entrance gate would be sought after, and rotating teams would be deployed to track all of his movements by car, train, or foot. Regular intercepts of Bauer's mail were authorized. The key would be identifying Bauer's new drop for Abramenkov. Past investigations had determined the GRU rarely used the same drop location more than once, or issued their agents a rotating list of sites. The beauty of the plan lied in its low risk but high reward design. As the plans would be false, the FBI would allow Abramenkov to clear the drop and believe his agent was still under his control and not the FBI's. In addition, feeding the Soviets false plans would be icing on the cake. Such plans could potentially set back their own research and design by years, giving the U.S. the upper hand in the space race. The plan was foolproof.

Chapter 61
New York City
Early 1953

Human nature, by design, demanded instant gratification. Counterespionage investigations were rarely instant, but could be extremely gratifying. Howard was at the pinnacle of his career as investigations such as Operation RED EYE were few and far between. A G-man's career could be made on such a case if he were successful. The BRAVE investigation had clearly drawn notice from FBIHQ from the beginning, catching Director Hoover's personal attention, and Howard's role as the lead investigator had propelled his career on a fast track. None of this was lost on Howard and he took his job very seriously. Howard was not in this for the accolades or awards. The American people had entrusted him with defending the front lines against the Soviet and Communist plague. The Soviets' brand of socialism threatened the very existence of our country's foundation built on the concepts of freedom and justice. During the war, Howard had defended his country with honor and almost with his life. He was not about to stop now and his pursuit was relentless.

Thus far, the surveillances of Bauer's weekend activities documented frequent trips from New Jersey to the NYU campus in New York. These trips were logical as Bauer had to prepare for and teach his undergraduate course. In addition, his son Johan had begun his studies at NYU studying architectural design, and shared an apartment nearby with three other NYU undergrads. Bauer's transportation from their home in West Orange to the NYU campus on Saturdays was always the same. He would often leave before 0800, stopping along the way at a local bakery to satisfy his sweet tooth and national heritage with the purchase of a strudel. Boarding the train near his home, Bauer would transfer in Jersey City, later arriving at Penn Station. Sometimes he would drive from home to Jersey City. From Penn, Bauer would often walk, weather permitting, but if not, he would hail a yellow cab. The team found it easy to follow Bauer because he often wore a hat with a brim more in line with a traditional Tyrolean hat than the standard fedora worn by most men. He also wore a light tan overcoat rather than the black type like most men traversing the city. These small differences distinguished Bauer in a crowd and allowed the team to create a bit of a gap, better preserving their anonymity.

The satellite project at Picatinny was codenamed PROJECT PATH and was progressing slowly after its launch in early April. Project briefs were provided by Johnson to Bauer and the other three researchers assigned to the team. Bauer was not removed from the atomic gun project, but Johnson saw to it that Bauer's role on PROJECT PATH was of more importance.

Not two weeks had passed before a letter was sent to Melvin Nowicki's post box in Queens. Nowicki continued to cooperate, not so much because of his fear of the FBI, but more so because of the respect Howard had afforded him from first contact. Respect was something Howard's parents had drilled into him from an early age, and Howard always afforded the same to anyone with whom he was in contact, friend or foe, until they gave him reason to take it away. Nowicki even continued his relationship ruse with Olga

Petrova. Fortunately, their interludes were infrequent, sparing Nowicki the pain of knowing he had betrayed his adopted country for the warmth of a deceptively cold woman.

Bauer's letter advised Abramenkov he would not be able to complete his previous work, referring to Abramenkov's tasking concerning the atomic gun, but promised a much better prize yet to come. The letter, although vague, meant Bauer had taken the bait, and it would only be a matter of time before he would be caught in the FBI's snare.

Chapter 62
New York City
May 1953

Day turned to night, and night to day, an inevitable cycle. The surveillances lingered on without results. The mail cover at Bauer's residence didn't produce anything out of the ordinary beyond the usual utility bills, such as NYU administrative notifications and common solicitations, advertising vacation and travel.

Johnson, Howard's mole inside Picatinny, didn't notice any abnormality in Bauer's routine or disposition. He remained a contributor but loner.

No new letters appeared in Nowicki's mailbox in Brooklyn.

Such was the norm in matters like this, long periods of tedium, rarely broken by action, waiting for the quarry to make a move. Howard regularly kept in touch with the many moving pieces of Operation RED EYE, aware that tedium could lead to complacency. Howard's time spent as an air crewman taught him this lesson.

He reminded the surveillance teams to keep up their vigilance looking for any slight changes in Bauer's work week and weekend routines. Coffee and donuts helped of course. Howard knew how to take care of his people, having been on the other end many times in the past. The team on Abramenkov kept their distance so not to spook him. This meant periods in which Abramenkov was in the wind and his activities went undetected.

Howard had to constantly talk his superiors at the New York Office and his minders at FBIHQ off the ledge. He had to reinforce the concept that Bauer was the real threat and the key to breaking Operation RED EYE. This was not an easy task. FBI men built their careers on results, especially those that caused splashy headlines. Howard felt his energy being drained by the constant interference. Such was the case, long periods of inactivity sometimes broken by surges of chaos.

Chapter 63
Picatinny Arsenal, NJ
May 1953 (Friday)

The PROJECT PATH team had begun preliminary drafts of a new propulsion system and fuel designed to lift a rocket suborbital by taking it about 62 miles above sea level. Johnson tempered their designs to create incremental results with each new design advancing the previous. Failures were to be expected, and the team experienced many. Johnson had to balance the appearance of success with the right amount of setbacks. Nevertheless, the excitement of pursuing such advances fueled the team's optimism, regardless how false the advances were.

In Bauer's case, he was both excited and disgusted. PROJECT PATH appealed to his personal and professional goals of being a leading rocket scientist. At an early age, he had been enthralled by radio programs and magazines in his home country of Germany that romanticized flight and the daring flyboys of World War I. But as he grew older and more mature, he quickly realized his gifts lied in the sciences. Besides, a car accident at an early age, resulting in damage to ligaments in his right knee, left him with a nagging stiffness and pain that he had learned to disguise remarkably well over the years. So, Bauer chose a lab coat, slide rule, and draftsman's table over a leather jacket and silk scarf. He knew his adventures would be made on the ground, and in many ways, be more rewarding.

However, along came a man who would change the course of German history. Adolf Hitler's accession to power was at first exciting and refreshing. His promotion of German superiority gave a beaten populous hope for the future. Hitler supported scientific achievement, and Germany once again found itself at the forefront of innovation. Bauer benefitted from Hitler's system, but greatly paid the price. Bauer was emerging as a leading scientist amongst his peers and his potential was unbound. But the German people were fooled by Hitler's "greatness," as his maniacal arrogance and blood thirsty zeal for vengeance soon caused the dreams of Bauer's and so many others to turn to nightmares. Bauer's work was for nothing, and he was prostituted to become another cog in the war machine. Bauer used his keen mind, exercised patience, and calculated his escape to American lines. He almost made it.

Now another mad man, who killed his own people, and was possibly a greater evil than Hitler himself, forced Bauer to again corrupt his scientific pursuits in support of a war, a cold war, possibly more dangerous than the last. Stalin and his henchmen threatened his family, his lovely bride Hanna, his beautiful sweet Gisela. So Bauer had no choice. He would perform like a circus clown for his Soviet handler Dmitry.

Bauer had finally accepted Abramenkov's demands. He use a Minox subminiature camera to take pictures instead of risking the removal of design blueprints. Bauer convinced Johnson he should work late to follow through on an inspired design thread for PROJECT PATH. Besides, Bauer explained, the other men had wives to go home to so he was the best positioned to put in a couple of extra hours. Johnson "accommodated" Bauer's request, leaving him alone in the lab with minimal staffing in the research department. Bauer waited patiently for the roving guard to make his sweep, giving Bauer about fifteen minutes without further risk.

Bauer hid his Minox camera in a false pocket inside his suit coat and left Picatinny. Bauer was unusually calm as he drove his 1950 Buick Roadmaster towards his home in West Orange. Maybe he had finally reached a point at which he had both successfully avoided detection as a spy for years, or he had finally resigned himself to the fact his life was controlled by others and he had no means or will to fight. Regardless of the reasons, for the first time, he enjoyed a sense of accomplishment without excruciating regret. As Bauer crossed Scotland Road, marking his arrival in his West Orange neighborhood and turned down Lawrence Avenue several blocks from his home, a route he had traversed hundreds of times over the past few years, he nearly rear ended the old Ford truck stopped in front of him at the traffic light. His near collision was not born from carelessness but from a simple vertical chalk mark affixed to the bottom of the corner post box. He stared at first with disbelief, which quickly gave way to utter panic. Abramenkov had set an emergency signal only to be used if Bauer was in dire danger.

Chapter 64
West Orange, NJ
May 1952

As he pulled to the curb in front of his home, Bauer's senses were in overdrive. He had to both emotionally and physically fight the ingrained human condition known as fight or flight. Every man, woman, and child he saw on his approach to his home was a threat. Did he see a single man standing in the shadows of Mrs. Baker's old sycamore tree? Was the old dented and rusted Chevrolet that passed him in the opposite direction as he turned the corner part of a surveillance team? Hadn't he seen that same car sitting outside the gates of Picatinny? Bauer told himself to breath deeply to calm his nerves. He then walked himself through the menial tasks of turning off the car, opening the door, stepping out with his left foot and then his right, and extracting himself from his car. He had to fight the internal debate raging in his head and the urge to swivel his head in every direction looking for confirmation he was being watched. He breathed in and out, in and out, and made his way to his front porch. Five steps, one foot after another, accomplished in less than four seconds, but what seemed like an eternity brought him to the front door. Bauer could barely get the key into the bolt lock as his hand was shaking with adrenaline coursing through his bloodstream. As he opened the door, he fully expected to be swarmed by a group of G-men, hell bent on making him pay for his treasonous life. But no one met him at the door, except the old calico cat now meandering between his legs. The house was empty and void of human warmth as it had been since Johan had left for college. Bauer collapsed on the couch and nearly passed out from relief, until he felt the small bulge in his jacket.

Chapter 65
Bauer's Home, West Orange, NJ
May 1952

By the following morning, Bauer had pulled himself together the best he could, given the circumstances. Sleep was elusive, but at least his nerves had calmed. After all, this may be a drill, he told himself, or at least something that would pass. As he lay in bed, Bauer ran through every move, every step he had taken in the past couple of years. Bauer could not pinpoint any one thing that would have caused him to be exposed. So he got up at the usual time, brushed his teeth, and took an extra long shower in an attempt to cleanse himself of guilt, or at least the appearance of guilt.

Once outside the house, Bauer followed his normal path to the bakery he often frequented on Saturday mornings. Prior to Friday night's events, he had planned to set a signal that morning alerting Abramenkov that he had the plans and would be making a drop. Instead, he hid the small roll of film inside the Arm and Hammer baking soda box inside the kitchen's refrigerator. The camera was returned to the concealment area under the floorboard in his bedroom's closet.

Undetected by Bauer, the FBI team was watching his every move. Bauer couldn't possibly have seen them, as they had a fixed observation post inside the upper floor of an old two-family residence across the street. One regular Bauer watcher was sitting inside a Greek diner, kitty corner to the bakery with an eye on the entrance and exit door. The team no longer followed Bauer into the bakery, having long ago established his Saturday morning routine.

Upon entering the bakery, Bauer was greeted warmly by the baker's wife, Mrs. Mueller, and they exchanged their typical greetings in their native German language. Mrs. Mueller asked about Johan and he provided her the latest. No, Johan had not found a special girl, and yes, he was as smart and gifted in academics as his father. Bauer believed the Muellers viewed him as a son, as their own had died on the horrendous streets of Stalingrad in the winter of 1942. Approaching the counter, Bauer placed his usual order for strudel and coffee, with the exception of asking for a half dozen extra for Johan. Why was Mr. Mueller averting his gaze? Or was Bauer just imagining so because of his precarious situation? That's odd, Bauer thought. Old man Mueller didn't ask about Johan nor did he mention the weather, something that was always on his mind. Bauer retrieved his sack of strudel and small coffee and headed for the exit. Pausing to grab a bite, he noticed the small piece of paper rolled inside. He immediately headed to the back of the bakery and into the bathroom normally reserved for the bakery's staff.

Bauer's hands shook, sticky with icing, as he unrolled the paper revealing Abramenkov's message. The note advised he was under FBI investigation and nearing arrest. Bauer was instructed to make his regular Saturday train ride that day into NYC to work and to visit his son. He was instructed to tell Johan he would be taking a business trip and would be out of town for a few days. Upon leaving for the day on the return train home, a man wearing an identical coat and hat and carrying the same satchel would be on board, immersed in a day old copy of The New York Times. Bauer was instructed to remove his own coat and hat and stuff them into the bathroom's waste basket at the end of the car. He was to stay in the bathroom and not exit at his usual stop while a decoy wearing the same hat and overcoat as Bauer exited the train and walked Bauer's usual route to his home. Bauer was to continue for two more stops, where he would exit and be met by a man holding a black umbrella and carrying a bag filled with two French baguettes. No further instructions were provided.

What Bauer wasn't told in the note by Abramenkov was the mysterious man, with the black umbrella and baguettes, was a fellow agent who would hide him for the night before taking him to the Sestroretsk, a relatively new Soviet cargo ship docked off Port Elizabeth in New Jersey. Bauer couldn't be made aware of the escape plan until he was under the watch of his handler/agent. Abramenkov feared Bauer would panic and flee, or alert Johan of his pending escape. As such, Bauer didn't get a chance to say a proper goodbye to his son.

Chapter 66
New Jersey
May 1952

The day started out uneventful as usual. Abramenkov emerged as expected with Tatiana for coffee and a buttered roll. But the unpredictable May skies quickly changed from cloudy to ominous, and a thunderous storm brought torrential rain. The Abramenkovs returned to their apartment and their watchers endured another spring soaking.

Sunday coverage was lighter than usual, and the team deployed in Bauer's neighborhood noted nothing of import beyond seeing movement and lights turning on and off the previous Saturday evening. Earlier on Saturday, Bauer had spent an hour at NYU, followed by his routine visit to Johan. The final Saturday log entry noted Bauer's bedroom light was extinguished short of midnight. Bauer did not emerge on Sunday, which wasn't alerting considering the foul weather. Sunday changed over to Monday as it had for hundreds of years.

However, by mid Monday morning, the team became concerned when Bauer didn't exit the house for his regular work day trip to Picatinny. Howard was contacted by the team at 1000, and he in turn contacted Johnson at Picatinny. Bauer had not called in sick, which Johnson thought strange as it was against Bauer's German sensibilities to let any detail go unchecked. The situation was briefed up as required. By early afternoon, a tremor of panic could be felt reverberating from the offices of the FBI executive management in New York and at FBIHQ. A decision was made to deploy a team member to Bauer's door dressed as a package courier. If Bauer was home and answered the door, the team member would "discover" he had the right house address, but wrong street. Panic increased when Bauer did not answer the door, and Howard went to West Orange to meet with the team.

From a nearby firehouse, Howard called Johnson and requested he personally call Bauer's home. The call went unanswered. Next, Howard contacted the West Orange police to conduct a ruse welfare check on behalf of Bauer's son Johan. Howard and the team met with the two uniformed officers sent to make contact and gave them enough information to know that Bauer was under the watch of the FBI. When their knocks went unanswered, First Class Police Officer Malcolm Henry, the larger of the two officers, drove his left shoulder into the front door, violently forcing it open. The door exploded and wood splinters filled the air. As Henry entered the living room and turned a corner towards the kitchen, he glimpsed a fast flurry of motion at the rear door leading out into the backyard. His years of experience unconsciously kicked in as he simultaneously yelled "backdoor" to his partner and gave chase. As Henry exited the same rear door, he saw a man finishing his climb over the backyard fence. Not breaking stride, he timed his leap and scaled the fence with ease. But the man had a decent lead and was already a good twenty yards ahead running through the alleyway at breakneck speed. As Henry pursued, he sensed his partner was only moments behind.

The impact of Bauer's front door exploding could be heard by the FBI team positioned down the block. At the time, Howard was talking with Agents Mark Kent and Danny

O'Malley outside their dark sedan about their next options. At the sound of the door and the yelling of the police officers, all started towards the house, but quickly changed direction as they saw a man running at full speed across Sycamore and disappear down the opposite alley. Kent and O'Malley started that way when they saw one of the two officers in close pursuit. As Kent and O'Malley followed on Henry's heals, Howard turned ninety degrees and sprinted down 3rd Street, parallel to the alleyway. Just as Howard hit the intersection at Maple Avenue, he glanced left to keep tabs on the pursuit, catching a glimpse of a large city transit bus heading in his direction.

Nothing prepared Howard for what came next. The fleeing man ran full speed in the path of the bus, its driver having no time to react. The impact was horrendous. Arms and legs flayed as human flesh hit the large chromed grill and then the pavement below. The screech of a mortally wounded animal came next as the front and rear wheels rolled over what was left of the prey. Stopping in shock at the unfolding scene, Howard saw Officer Kelly, Henry's partner, Kent and O'Malley all sliding to a stop short of the bus's path, their mouths agape with shock and horror. Howard regained his senses just enough to jog towards the splayed and unmoving man. As Howard approached, he quickly noticed two things. The bus driver was sitting in the cab in utter shock, his face pale and almost grey. And... the man was not Bauer.

Shock turned to confusion, confusion turned to training and procedure. A search of Bauer's residence produced only Bauer's old calico cat, found pacing back and forth at his bowl in the kitchen. All, including Howard, now headed into full panic mode. Although all possible logical locations had to be checked for Bauer, the implications of the incident at Bauer's residence were clear. Bauer was gone, not just missing.

Chapter 67
New York City
May 1952

Fran's surprise of Howard visiting her office at NYU's University Heights undergraduate campus in the Bronx during a weekday was, at first, a wonderful surprise. However, her surprise quickly turned from pleasure to confusion at the sight of Howard's distraught face. Howard's request of Fran to check with NYU officials, and personally reach out to Johan, transitioned the situation from confusion to concern.

"Francis, listen, I can't explain anything further. Please trust me on this and maybe I will be able to explain everything someday," Howard asked, nearly pleading. Fran had never seen Howard so stressed, a remarkable departure from his usual quiet but confident manner. Howard never called Fran by her full first name, always choosing to use one of many affectionate pet names.

"Howard, it's okay. I can tell Professor McKinney that I need to head down to our Washington Square campus to prepare a lecture and reception for this next Thursday," Fran replied, setting Howard a bit at ease. Riding in the FBI sedan with one of Howard's fellow agents would have been a bit of a thrill if not for her concern for Howard and what he must be experiencing.

After checking in with the Administrative Department and the Adjunct Office for any messages concerning Bauer, Fran returned to the dark sedan and informed its driver, SA Ed Hurst, that no one had heard from Bauer. During the short ride to Johan's apartment, Fran's mind flipped somersaults wondering what was so important about Bauer's whereabouts. Of course, she was feeling the appropriate amount of concern for a missing colleague, but the FBI's involvement, and in particular, Howard's personal involvement was bewildering.

Hurst pulled the dark sedan to the curb well short of the apartment house identified as Johan's, and Fran exited the car nervously straightening her skirt as she composed herself. Fran walked up the three flights to Johan's floor, and as she approached the door, she paused to take a few cleansing breaths to control her heartbeat. Having spent a lifetime focused on the sciences and not the arts, Fran was nervous about how she would perform, especially without a script. Just as Fran started to knock on the door, the door immediately swung open, startling Fran. A younger and thinner version of Bauer himself appeared at the door wearing a coat and hat, obviously set to head out. The young man was equally startled himself.

"I'm sorry, I didn't expect anyone to be on the other side of the door," the young man exclaimed, catching his breath, with a smile starting to nervously form on his face.

"No, I'm the one who should be sorry," Fran said as she recovered from her shock. "My name is Fran Brooks and I work at NYU. I'm looking for a Johan Bauer, son of Wilhem Bauer, a colleague of mine.

"Well, you have found him. I'm Johan," he replied with forming tension on his face at the mention of his father who hadn't called him Sunday evening as usual. "What's this about my father?" Johan asked.

Sensing Johan's building alarm, Fran quickly smiled to set Johan at ease. "Sorry Johan, it appears I've caused you some distress. Your father Wilhelm and I work together in the Physics Department. He had left a message at our office that he had left behind some papers at your apartment when he last visited. He asked that I drop by to pick them up and deliver them to Professor Newberry," Fran explained, following the thin script provided by Howard. "I see you're on your way out, so if I could just get what he had left behind, I'll be on my way."

"That's funny, I don't remember my father leaving anything behind. He's usually very careful with his belongings, but please come in and I will check around," Johan replied holding the door open for Fran.

Once inside, Johan conducted a quick search of the small combined living room and kitchenette. The apartment was remarkably neat for a college apartment and nothing appeared out of the place. Sensing Johan's search was coming to an end, Fran asked, "When was your father last here to visit?"

"Just this past Saturday as usual. My father and I usually have an early dinner after his afternoon lecture," Johan remarked somewhat distantly as he recalled the weekend. "Oddly, he didn't phone last night as usual. He has forgotten before after dozing off in his reading chair. I would ring him at work for you, but he told me he was going out of town on business through Thursday," Johan offered.

"Oh, please don't bother, really. He must be mistaken about leaving the papers here. Perhaps he left them behind in the office after all. I will call him myself. Thank you and sorry to have held you up," Fran quickly offered as she turned towards the door.

"Wait, and I will walk out with you. In fact, I'm heading over to the campus right now. We can walk together," Johan said as he turned the lock and closed the door behind them.

The walk with Johan was short in distance but felt long in duration. They made small talk about Johan's studies and Fran's position at NYU as they walked past Hurst's sedan. Fran noticed Ed was not behind the wheel as she stole a glance. As they arrived at Washington Square, Fran made an excuse that she had to run a quick errand and bid her goodbyes to Johan. She watched him walk away with the energy of youth, carefree and exited about the future. Fran was beginning to worry about this affair with Johan's father. What is going on? She wondered as she turned back towards the FBI sedan. Most importantly, why was Howard involved?

Chapter 68
The Fallout
1952

After getting no further ahead by contacting Johan, the seriousness of the situation increased exponentially. A witch hunt ensued. As a result of Bauer's disappearance, Hoover deployed a team from FBIHQ to New York by that following Wednesday, including Jack, to launch an investigation of Operation RED EYE and the involved personnel. The FBI NYO team was told to stand-down and all were questioned. Howard was questioned the hardest, as he, of course, was central to the affair. Howard endured numerous rounds of questioning over his management of the case, and his abilities and leadership were called into question. Robinson inserted himself demanding the investigators listen to reason and attempted to take the heat himself. But to no avail. A mole hunt ensued and no one escaped its taint.

The Picatinny staff was questioned and Johnson later recalled it a disgusting period in its history. Of course, Bauer was not out of town on company business. The sham project was shut down immediately, and when the U.S. Government actually advertised for design bids for research and development, Picatinny excused itself, as the bitterness of the affair remained palatable.

While the investigation continued, Howard and the other team members were relegated to benign surveillances of low level Soviet officials and endless paperwork surrounding Operation RED EYE. Almost as an afterthought, Howard personally reached out to his source Melvin Nowicki. Nowicki could not be found at home and a search of his mailbox produced days' old mail. A canvas of co-workers revealed that most last saw Bauer on the past Friday, as he didn't show for work on the following Monday morning. A surreptitious search of his residence produced nothing of import. He seemed to have disappeared into thin air.

Abramenkov and Tatiana didn't emerge the weekend of Bauer's disappearance. After all, the weather was foul. A week following Bauer's disappearance, the FBI intercepted a letter from Moscow indicating Tatiana's father had died. By the following Saturday, the Abramenkovs boarded a plane to Moscow, by way of Vienna, apparently to return to handle personal affairs. However, they never returned, bolstering the FBI's suspicions concerning a mole.

Olga Petrova's outings ceased all together and a search of boarding records revealed she had left the day prior to the Abramenkovs.

Weeks dragged on as Howard and the rest of the team were relegated to office duties. Howard was apologetic to the team and demanded the focus and any fault be assessed to him alone. Each stood by Howard and offered their support. Jack didn't outright accuse Howard of complicity, but personally led the mole investigation. Months passed without results.

A timeline of events was ordered, prepared, and later used to hang the accused. Hoover's team issued a report documenting a number of failings concerning RED EYE, including lax surveillances, a decision to only focus on BRAVE and not Abramenkov, and presumed missed signs of BRAVE's awareness he was under scrutiny. As the team lead, Howard became the scapegoat for most of the report's findings. As a result, he was temporarily re-assigned to conducting background investigations on applicants for special agent positions and for senior White House appointees.

The affair passed and work returned to some normalcy. Outwardly, Howard returned to the work of defending the U.S. from the Soviet plague and spending the next few years salvaging his career in Counterespionage. Privately, Howard never stopped looking for clues about what went wrong. What had Howard missed? Who or what tipped off Bauer to the FBI's investigation? Did Abramenkov make the teams and the connection to Bauer? Was the Picatinny ruse project too transparent, or had Abramenkov seen it as a provocation? Howard knew Bauer couldn't have disappeared without assistance, well-placed, and resourceful. These thoughts dominated his mind.

Sadly, several months later, Nowicki's body was found in the water, pinned between a pier footing and dry dock gate at the Brooklyn Navy Yards. Finding water in his lungs and a small metal flask of cheap whiskey in an inside coat pocket, the New York Police Department Medical Examiner concluded the cause of death was drowning. The FBI didn't acknowledge his status as one of their sources and he was buried in a modest plot in Potter's Field on Hart Island after a brief Russian Orthodox ceremony attended by only a few Navy Yard co-workers and fellow bar patrons. One man wearing a dark suit, drab overcoat, and well worn fedora stood off to the side. Howard's gut told him Nowicki's death was not accident.

After time, the love of a beautiful supportive wife and the birth of a healthy baby boy, full of wonder and hope, become the ointment to heal Howard's wounds. Slowly, Howard put the matter behind him. But the mystery concerning what happened lingered in the recesses of his mind. Two years later, in the fall of 1954, Robinson took a promotion and transferred to Washington, DC. Howard became a leading candidate for Robinson's desk, and with Robinson's undying support at FBIHQ, Howard was promoted to lead his own Soviet squad.

Some confusion remained over why Bauer had told his only son he was going out of town on business. Had he done so to buy time and distance himself from the FBI? Did he even know that he was going to disappear?

Chapter 69
Sun City West, Arizona
July 1985

Howard pulled the rental car to the curb, parking short of the single story house, and surveyed his surroundings. Old habits die hard. The house looked like all the others on the street, earthen colored, adobe style, built en masse as thousands moved to the desert seeking quiet refuge in retirement. In the late 1950's, Jack had left FBIHQ taking a supervisor's desk in the Phoenix Field Office, which had been established in the valley in the late 1930's. Twice divorced, he had retired in the early 1970's, settling in a planned community in the Phoenix valley.

Howard and Jack had minimally kept in touch over the years, and even that was mainly while Jack was still at FBIHQ working Counterespionage. Howard had followed Jack and his periodic exploits over the years. As organized crime emerged as a national concern in the 1950's, Jack and others in the Phoenix Division joined the fight against the mob. In the late 1950's, mobsters such as Joe Bonanno, Jr. moved to Arizona. Bonanno settled in Tucson, and was later arrested by Jack and others for obstructing a grand jury investigation against his sons. Besides Bonanno, other Mafia members moved to Arizona in the 1950's and 1960's, such as Charles Joseph Battaglia, Jr., who for years often avoided jail because witnesses were unwilling to testify against him. In a third major Phoenix mob case, Eugene Bulgarino and 19 associates were charged with robbery, extortion, gambling, bribery, and drug and firearms offenses. Sixteen subjects pled guilty by the conclusion of the case. The warm air and forever blue skies must have been the draw, or maybe it was the lure of the "Wild Wild West."

Howard sat in his car, pausing to gather his thoughts. The heat was blistering, and as Howard looked up the slight elevation rise towards the distant desert mountains, he could see a shimmer hovering above the asphalt, warning those who would tread upon it. Ever since the visit Howard received by Agents Gallow and Kowolski at his home in Florida, Howard was no longer able to suppress his memories and theory about the BRAVE investigation into the back recesses of his mind. Once only a faint nagging distraction during times of quiet solitude, they were now pervasive and unrelenting. They demanded attention.

Howard pulled his tired bones from the rented sedan, planted both feet firmly, and fixed a steady stride towards the front door, no longer able to avoid destiny. A wave of heat, dry heat as the locals always offered, hit Howard square in the face. Howard's knock went unanswered the first and second times, but on the third attempt to rouse the occupant, the door opened to reveal his old and once dearest friend.

"Rarely do I have visitors anymore," Jack said with a tired pronouncement, as he stepped to the side inviting Howard across the door's threshold. Howard entered without exchanging any greetings, as none were expected. "I knew some day you would pay a visit. I only expected it would be much sooner," Jack said as he walked past Howard to a small bar along the back wall. As he poured himself two fingers worth of Jack Daniels, Jack offered the same to Howard by holding up the bottle with a quizzical look fixed on his face. "Well, I suppose not," he said.

"Jack, Tom Conrad sent two agents from headquarters to my home to ask me about the RED EYE investigation," Howard said, directly to the point and void of pleasantries.

"Well, it was only a matter of time I suppose," Jack replied. "At least they could have paid me the same courtesy, but I guess that means something, doesn't it, Howard?" Jack stated rhetorically, more as a fact than a question. "How is Fran, Howard?"

"She's fine, thank you. I didn't tell her I was going to visit you, but I'm sure she suspects. She probably knew she couldn't stop me anyway," Howard said as he turned toward the large living room window and stared out across the expansive desert landscape, only marred by new homes in various degrees of construction. Without turning to face Jack, Howard asked one simple question. "Why Jack?"

"It's simple, really Howard," Jack said followed by a small sip of the amber liquid. "She was my first and last love, Howard, only I couldn't have her. You remember that first time you visited me in New York, don't you Howard? When you were undecided about where your life was heading? You arrived early by train and Ms. Voronov, my landlady, let you in. She and her daughter Viktoriya lived on the ground floor. Viktoriya drew me in like no other woman, Howard. The moment I laid eyes on her beautiful and flawless face, her ample bosom, and the curve at the small of her back, I was smitten. But as they say, beauty is only skin deep. Except, in her case, her beauty lied deep in her heart, in her soul. She was exceptional in every way Howard. She was my Fran, I suppose. Our passion was real but not meant to be. How could it, Howard? As you'll recall, we were at the forefront of battling the Communist menace. Our hot war, the one you and I had put our lives on the line for, was over. But our cold war was just beginning; only it was against a foe we had called friend just months before. I had deeply fallen for Viktoriya and I gave into my desires even though I knew it was wrong. After all Howard, I was working Soviet Counterespionage in the largest FBI office, our flagship, wasn't I? If the Bureau ever found out about my transgressions, I would have been caught up in the world wind of suspicions launched so carelessly at the time, and locked away forever. I was a good agent, a patriot Howard. Only things got complicated, real fast. Viktoriya became pregnant and I knew it was mine. Her mother was distraught and sent her to live with relatives in Brighton Beach. I knew from our investigations that her aunt and uncle were on our list of CPUSA members. Viktoriya gave birth to a beautiful little girl with faint blue eyes and hair the color of straw. Improbably, she was more beautiful than her mother, Howard. At first, I thought I could find a way to work things out. Have both Viktoriya and our little Katherina in my life. But others within the CPUSA found out about my predicament, and one day I received a letter under my apartment door which would change my life. Not only would I not have Viktoriya and Katherina in my life, I would never lead a normal life after that day. I think you can work out the rest of the details and complete the story Howard, if they are really even important anymore. After all, these days, new threats have taken precedent over the Communist plague. The Soviet Union is only a shell of its former self. We have won that war, Howard, if you can really call it that," Jack finished as he drained his drink and started to pour another. Howard noticed the small tremor in Jack's hands starting to ease.

As Howard stood at the window, flashes of memories long suppressed sped through his mind and now all made sense. His underlying, but never acknowledged, suspicions were now confirmed. Jack sitting in the dark sedan down the street from the Pharmacy as the Abramenkovs walked passed and "disappeared." Bauer exchanging the package of the Atomic Cannon materials with Abramenkov behind the Christmas tree in Rockefeller Plaza as Jack held the "eye" ensuring the team missed the brush pass. Jack's tip off of Bauer's looming arrest through Abramenkov's note at the bakery. In some small way, Howard understood it all. Jack's "Fran" said it all. How wrenching it all must have been for Jack to be denied his true love.

Howard turned from the window and their eyes locked for a few moments as each acknowledged each other's divergent destinies. With a small nod, Howard walked to the door without looking back and passed over the threshold back into the oppressive heat, drained of energy but clear of mind. Starting the car, Howard rolled down the windows to let the heat escape. As he shifted the car into gear and started to roll down the hill, past the single story adobe, a single muffled shot could be heard, unmistakable to a career FBI man.

Epilogue
Unfinished Business

Nearly two weeks aboard a Soviet freighter grated on Bauer's nerves and nearly pushed him over the edge. Abandoning his son Johan nearly suffocated Bauer from stress. However, his yearning to feel the warm skin of his wife Hanna and to look into the eyes of his lost daughter Gisela kept Bauer from going fully insane from grief. Arriving in Moscow, Bauer didn't expect a hero's welcome, so his reception was not disappointing. He was met unceremoniously by two GRU heavies and escorted to their headquarters at the Khodinka Airfield for a meeting with Colonel Sergei Shtemenko, his puppet master of all these many years. Entering the finely appointed and opulent office in a newly provided but ill fitting suit, Bauer was met by Dmitry Abramenkov. For the first time, their meeting was not a hurried and brief affair, and neither had to look over their shoulders for the FBI. Colonel Shtemenko entered the room followed by a uniformed aide. Shtemenko presented Bauer with an award for Soviet bravery and distinction. A few words were spoken and Shtemenko took leave as quickly as he had entered. Bauer was left standing with Abramenkov, confused and dazed. He had expected to be reunited with Hanna and Gisela. Why weren't they at the ceremony? Turning towards Abramenkov, Bauer started to open his mouth and form the words, but he could see in Abramenkov's eyes his answer. His world came crashing down all around him both mentally and physically. Falling to his knees, he began to weep uncontrollably. He barely felt his escorts lifting him by the arms and dragging his body from the room. Two days later, Bauer took his life by hanging himself in his sparse dacha located just outside Moscow.

Following his father's disappearance, Johan was questioned at length and his apartment searched repeatedly. At first, he was led to believe an investigation of his father's disappearance was a standard affair. After all, a respected member of the NYU community and a government facility had disappeared without a trace. Johan invited the FBI's involvement. However, he soon grew suspicious and demanded answers. In the end, he was told his father was a Soviet agent and had committed treason against his adopted country. Johan publically denied that fact and remained an undying advocate for his father's name. Privately, he suspected the allegations were true. In 1969, his suspicions were confirmed with the receipt of a cryptic letter from his father written a couple of weeks after his disappearance in 1952. In the letter, a father apologized to his son for his failings. Johan never heard from his father again and would never know the true fate of his mother and sister. Johan didn't care who had forwarded the letter after all these many years.

Dmitry Abramenkov and his lovely Tatiana, with their tour in New York cut short, spent the next year in Moscow before being assigned to Dmitry's next posting in Vienna. Having both successfully handled Bauer and an FBI Agent in New York, Dmitry's future was bright.

The FBI's reinvestigation into the BRAVE affair was closed without final disposition; Howard had learned from Tom Conrad outside a small Methodist church in rural Iowa. In his last act of friendship, Howard didn't share with Tom or Fran what he had learned from the man now laid to rest in the modest family plot. Neither spoke of Howard's visit to Jack on that hot late morning in July, but Tom suspected. They departed with a friendly handshake and promises to keep in touch. Both knew the promises to be a hallow, as neither wanted to acknowledge what had really happened all those years ago. But both knew, and the BRAVE matter was now laid to rest in a modest family plot outside a small town in rural Iowa.

Afterword

Thank you for choosing to read my first novel Enemy Past. Historical novels generally have two things in common, a story line featuring prominent historical events and characters, and fictional departures from that very history. Many of the people, places and events you read in Enemy Past are true or based on true events. Here are some truths.

The 390th Bomber Group, comprised of the 568th, 569th, 570th, and 571st Squadrons, was a real bomber group activated as part of the United States 8th Army Air Force in 1943. In July of that same year, the Group's air and ground troops were dispatched to Suffolk, England and based at Station 153, Framlingham. The 390th flew its first mission on August 12, 1943, and its 301st and last mission on April 20, 1945. The 390th's B-17 "Flying Fortresses" bombed aircraft factories, bridges, and oil refineries, and received the Presidential Unit Citation for its efforts. In addition, the 390th broke a record for enemy aircraft destroyed by any one group on any one mission by destroying sixty-two at Munster on October 10, 1943. In total, the 390th Bomber Group destroyed 377 enemy aircraft and recorded fifty-seven "probable's" and seventy-seven damaged. And, they were never turned back by the enemy. A total of 714 390th airmen sacrificed their lives in the cause of freedom.

Technical Sgt. Howard K. Brooks, a small town kid from the very small town of Otho, was a Radio Operator and Gunner with the 390th. Howard was also my paternal Grandmother's brother, and my Great Uncle. The Liberty Belle was a B-17G "Flying Fortress" assigned to the 390th. Howard flew 28 missions with Crew 64, all but seven aboard the Liberty Belle. On February 14, 1945, Crew 64, piloted by Lieutenants Don Hassig and Howard Sackett, participated in a bombing mission to Cheb, Czechoslovakia. And, on her return flight, the Liberty Belle was severely damaged by German flak; although her courageous pilots managed to keep the aircraft aloft all the way to Belgium.

The New York Office of the FBI and its Counterespionage and Counterintelligence programs are well known to both the studied and casual historian. One can find many true accounts of the investigations and arrests of famous Nazi and Soviet spies. The New York Office led many of these famous cases. Former Director Hoover's personal micromanagement of his field offices is well known by the men who served under him during his nearly 48 years of service. His fight against Communism is legendary, or infamous, depending on your viewpoint.

The streets and buildings defining New York University's historic Washington Square campus are generally consistent with the 1950's. Discrepancies very well could exist, as current and openly available information of its structure during the period of the 1940's through 1960's is somewhat vague. Visiting the campus today, one would still be at a loss to know they were on the campus of a major U.S. University if not for the lavender colored flags which identify current NYU offices, libraries, and academic buildings.

In addition, readily available information concerning the exact location of the Soviet Mission in the 1950's is also a bit sketchy. Even so, I don't think this should distract from the story.

But like all historical novels, Enemy Past departs along some very major plot lines. In Enemy Past, my Great Uncle Howard recovers from his injuries sustained during the bombing mission to Cheb, returns home, seeks a college education, and embarks on a grand adventure to New York City. Howard pursues an honorable and worthwhile career in the FBI, and meets the love of his life, Fran. However, here lies a great departure from reality.

Like so many young men who went off to war to fight for freedom, Howard did not return home to his family. He did not get a chance to earn a college education through the G.I. Bill and build a rewarding career, nor did he have a chance to build a life with his new bride and start a family. Instead, Howard succumbed to his mortal wounds aboard the Liberty Belle, and was officially pronounced dead upon their tenuous landing on February 14, 1945. Howard was temporarily interned at a U.S. Cemetery in Belgium called Henri-Chapelle before his remains were recovered by his loving family and returned to Otho, Iowa. Howard was laid to rest in a family plot, in a small and rolling rural cemetery just outside of Otho.

I should note that, like many young men caught up in the urgency of the time, Howard met and fell in love with a local young woman named Mae while Howard was attending Radio Operator's school in Sioux Falls, South Dakota. While on leave and just before departing for England, Howard and Mae wed with a promise to hold each other dear in their thoughts and actions. For plot convenience, I changed their relationship to include Mae breaking off their relationship. I meant no offense towards Mae or her family. Mae moved on with her life, and later remarried like so many young war widows. May God bless Mae and her family no matter where life took her.

A major reason for writing Enemy Past was to give Howard an opportunity to live a life he would never know. In giving Howard a life filled with love and meaningful work, I wrote this book to represent all the other young men and women who served their country with distinction and honor. Young men, full of dreams and aspirations, who paid the ultimate sacrifice so you and I could fulfill our own dreams. I would like to believe that Howard could have chosen a life dedicated to the further defense of his country through service in the FBI, and found meaning in its pursuit.

Before you go, I would implore you to check out two wonderful museums dedicated to the memory of the men of the 390th Bomber Group. After returning from the war, the men of the 390th soon began hold regular reunions. Later, these same veterans, their families, and many wishing to honor their sacrifice and memory formed an association and built the 390th Memorial Museum on the grounds of the Pima Air & Space Museum in Tucson, Az. Also, if you ever find yourself across the pond, take time to visit the 390th Bombardment Group Memorial Air Museum and Museum of the British Resistance Organisation housed in the restored Control Tower at Framingham 153, Parham, England. Please visit their websites for additional information.

Made in the USA
Middletown, DE
01 August 2016